Match Me

Other Books by AJ Adaire

Don't Forget

Journey To You

I Love My Life

It's Complicated

One Day Longer Than Forever

Friend Series
Sunset Island - Book 1
The Interim (a novelette)
Awaiting My Assignment - Book 2
Anything Your Heart Desires - Book 3

Match Me

AJ Adaire

Desert Palm Press

Match Me

By AJ Adaire

©2018 AJ Adaire

(trade) ISBN: 9781942976950
(ebook) ISBN: 9781942976967
(pdf) ISBN: 9781942976974

Desert Palm Press
1961 Main Street, Suite 220
Watsonville, California 95076
www.desertpalmpress.com

Editor: CK King
Cover Design: AJ Adaire
Photo Credits: Kraft2727/depositphotos.com; interact images/depositphotos.com; ariadnaS/depositphotos.com

Printed in the United States of America
First Edition June 2018

Acknowledgement

This book has passed through many hands on its way to you, the reader. I'd like to thank the following people: Irene, who allows me the time I need to write; my beta readers who've combed through and commented to make this story the best it can be; C.K. King, my editor, who polishes and reorganizes my words until they shine their best; and finally my publisher, Lee, who pulls it all together and gets it to you, the reader. Lastly, thank you to all my readers, for supporting my work over these past years.

Dedication

To my mother, a very funny woman, who was the inspiration for Grams and her friend, Millie. Although my mother didn't always approve, I know she loved me unconditionally. Thanks, Mom.

CHAPTER ONE

"CAN I STAY WITH you?" Mica Baxter sat on the bed, phone to her ear, and leaned against the last of the suitcases she'd packed that morning.

"Hang on a minute." Casey Harrison glanced over at Haley, her current girlfriend, and moved into the kitchen, hopefully out of earshot. "What's up?"

"I've had it. I can't do this anymore. I can't take the moods, the jealousy, the accusations."

"Is she there with you now?"

"No, thank God." Mica played with the toggle on the bag zipper. "I told her I was leaving, and she stormed out. I'll rent an apartment as soon as possible, so I can get out from under your feet."

"Sure, Mica. The spare room is all yours for as long as you need it." She leaned over and checked on Haley's location. Casey lowered her voice. "I'd welcome having someone here who likes the same things I do. You bringing your stuff over now?"

Mica glanced around at the stacked bags. "Within the hour. I still need to lug everything to the car. I can't believe I'm homeless, again."

"You're not homeless. You always have a place with me."

Haley came around the corner just as Casey ended the call with her friend. "Who has a place with you?"

"Uh...Mica." Casey prepared for the tirade.

Haley rolled her eyes. "A place. You mean here with us?"

"It won't be for long." Casey chose to ignore the 'with us' comment since, technically, Haley didn't live with her full time. She only stayed with Casey Friday through Sunday. Because she worked in the city and hated the commute, Haley kept a room at a friend's house for the weekdays.

"Five minutes with her is too long. You two gang up against me all the time. You and Mica like the same music, the same TV shows, and have the same sarcastic sense of humor. It feels like you two are the couple and I'm an outsider."

"Don't be ridiculous. We've been friends for like...well forever."

Casey stuck her phone back into her pocket. "I've told you a million times, you've no reason to be jealous of her."

"I think thou dost protest too much." Haley's fingers drummed against her thigh.

"Oh, for God's sake! I'm not protesting. I'm denying. If we were ever going to have been a couple, don't you think it would have happened by now?"

Haley's nostrils flared. "If she's coming now, I'm going home. I really want to see that movie we planned to watch." Haley put her hand on her hip and stuck out her bottom lip. "It's my weekend to choose. Even if I'm not overruled, the two of you will ruin it for me by making fun of everything."

"I'm sorry, I don't understand how anyone can watch monster movies and not see the humor in them. Seriously, how can you not laugh at a giant lizard terrorizing a city?"

"They're not comedies. They're meant to frighten you. All you do is make fun and laugh."

In her heart, Casey knew Haley had a valid point. At the outset of her relationship with Haley, at the point when the sex was hot, and the differences mattered less, they'd both been more tolerant of their diverse likes and dislikes. Lately, they'd been arguing about things as minute as the toilet paper over/under debate, and whether the knives should face left or right in the silverware tray. Even meals were a challenge. Casey was a devoted carnivore, and Haley an avowed vegan who hated the smell of meat.

Back in the living room, the two women retreated to separate ends of the sofa. Haley narrowed her eyes and glared in Casey's direction. "Do I not have any say in her staying here?"

Noting the arch in Haley's eyebrow, Casey was wary of where this discussion was headed. She bit back her immediate no response in favor of a more reasonable approach. "Look, what would you have me say to her? She's my oldest friend, my business partner, and..." She almost said, 'I love her.' Although the last statement was true, Casey knew it would elicit a tirade she really didn't want to deal with today. They were treading on rocky ground already, so she simply said, "my best friend."

"Yes. I've heard all those things before." Haley walked to the closet and took out her coat.

Casey's eyebrows lowered creating a frown line between them. "What are you doing?"

Haley picked up the bag she carried back and forth every weekend and set it next to the door. She always packed on Sunday morning and put her things into the closet, to be ready for her trip back to the city on Sunday evening. "I'm going home. One day this week, when you're not here, I'll come for the rest of my things. You'll find my key on the table then." Haley's lips were set firmly together. "I think whatever this was has run its course. Don't you?"

"Are you really leaving because Mica is coming to stay here? I told you it'll only be for a short time." Casey approached her angry girlfriend.

Raising a hand indicating stop, Haley shook her head and stalled Casey's forward progress. "That's only part of it, and you know it. We've been in a relationship for months. I don't feel like I know any more about who you are than I did at the end of our first two weeks of dating. I feel like I'm always less—less important than work, less important than your grandmother, less important than your friends. You're a closed person, Casey. You keep people at a distance. Somehow, Mica got in."

"Come on, Haley. Mica's been a friend…"

"I know…forever. I've heard that before. Think about it. You're an attractive woman with a great personality and good sense of humor. You never have trouble getting a lover. You don't manage to hang onto them though. You've had a series of relationships that all ended the same way. You don't commit to your lover half as deeply as you do to your friends, especially to Mica."

"Haley…"

"I suspect you'll probably attribute the end of our relationship to me being jealous. It's not that. By nature, I'm not a jealous or unkind person. Maybe it's as simple as we're not the right people for each other." She shrugged. "One thing I am sure about, is that I need more from my lover than you're willing to give. I need someone able to be open enough to risk their heart." Haley picked up her bag and turned to kiss Casey on the cheek. "I'm sorry Casey. This isn't working for me. I hope you'll find what you need someday."

Casey stood staring at the door. Her mind raced as she tried to figure out what had just happened. Haley was right about one thing. Casey was a failure at long-term relationships. Her romantic track record was dismal and discouraging. Although not all of them ended up being sexual, she'd had more short-term relationships than a bank teller at a drive through. Of all the breakups over the years, ever since Jennifer, this one with Haley had been the most civilized. Casey sighed and returned to the living room, where she poured herself a sherry and carried it to the sofa.

The sound of the doorbell caused Casey to jump. For a second, she thought that maybe, Haley had returned. Instead, Mica opened the door and stood there surrounded by three suitcases. "I have more in the car. Want to help me carry them up?"

CHAPTER TWO

CASEY HURRIED TO HER car. She was on her way to meet Mica, who had moved into her own apartment on a cold, rainy Saturday about six weeks after she'd shown up with her pile of suitcases. That was about eight months ago. Mica having her own apartment made as much sense as a stripper having an extensive wardrobe. Except for Mica going home to sleep, it seemed that the two friends were always together.

Mica was already inside when Casey pulled into the diner's parking lot. She hurried up the steps and spied Mica in a booth against the wall. Casey gave Mica's shoulder a quick squeeze and slid into the vinyl seat opposite her.

"Hey, look at this, Casey." Mica slid the newspaper across the slightly sticky table in their favorite breakfast joint and tapped her finger on the quarter-page advertisement. "We could use a vacation, don't ya think?"

Casey squinted as she read aloud. "Win a romantic adventure for two on a private island. Gorgeous views, isolated living, plus four days in Key West in luxurious accommodations. What's that about?"

"Forget the romantic part. Think sand, sea, and cool breezes. Wouldn't it be neat to be on a private island for a week with your best friend? Plus, there's a few days at a resort before and after. Please, please, please? If you do this for me, I'll owe you big time. You get to name the price."

"Did you read the description of the island? It's described as rustic. That can't be good, although it does say all expenses paid." A long sigh escaped Casey's lips. "What hoops do you have to jump through to win?"

"Hmm...looks like it's a new lesbian dating service named Match Me opening up. They are trying to recruit folks, so they're offering one free membership and a fifty percent discount if you join with a friend. The rules say that you're each required to accept a minimum of one date from the list they send you to be eligible for the vacation drawing. All the details of the date are arranged by them. They send you the person's name, a meeting location, and the time. Doesn't that sound like fun?"

"I'd suspect my last root canal might have been more fun than either of us will have on a computer-matched date. What could a computer know about my taste in female companionship?"

"You'll never know until you try. Come on, Casey, how many dates have you had in the last six months using your real-world charm and assets?" Mica's eyes took in the visible length of her friend.

"I don't need dates. I have you." Casey's fingers slid through her hair, as she rolled her eyes. "Why? Why do I let you talk me into these things? Last time it was that Dumb Mudder thing. We damned near drowned in the electrified mud pit. I think my back still carries the mark where the electric wire stung me."

"That's not what it's called, and you know it. Besides, I told you not to crawl on your hands and knees. You have to slither like a rattler."

"Slither like a rattler. Yeah, right. It was embarrassing. Admit it, Mica. You and I were the oldest people there. We took a lot of ribbing from all those young kids."

"Complain all you like. At least you finished."

"I was last."

"You were only one step behind me. I was proud of us. Come on. Wouldn't you like to meet someone and settle down?"

"I guess. What would I do with you?" Casey winked at Mica. "We've been friends since right after high school. We went to the same college, and now we own a business together. For the ten months we've both been single, we work together all day and spend every night with each other. I don't think either of us has been actively looking for a date. Hell, if we do meet someone who shows a scintilla of interest in one of us, we ask them to bring a friend and we double date. We're like forty-two-year-old teenagers."

"That's even more reason to give this a chance. Who knows, maybe we'll meet the woman of our dreams and have a wonderful vacation." As Casey attempted to interrupt, Mica raised a finger. "I know, I know, you think it's a dumb idea with absolutely zero chance of success. Assume you're right...that the computer can't offer up a perfect woman for either of us. If one of us wins the trip, we can go together and have a free, all-expense-paid trip. Come on, be a sport." Mica kicked Casey's leg under the table. "Please? And none of those long, tortured sighs. Just nod."

Casey sobered for a second, as the thought raced through her head. *Suppose there is a perfect woman for one of us. What then?* Near capitulation, Casey again rolled her eyes and shook her head left to right.

"Your grandmother would say, 'If you keep rolling those eyes like that, they'll get stuck that way forever.' Anyway, you're shaking your head in the wrong direction…it should go up and down, like this." Mica demonstrated with an exaggerated nod.

Casey took another deep breath and exhaled it audibly.

"That's about the fifth big sigh. If you keep heaving out those huge gulps of air, I'm going to have to get you a paper bag to breathe into."

"I'm not hyperventilating." Casey shook her head. "You're impossible."

"Come on, Case, be a sport."

Contrary to Mica's admonishment, a long and breathy sigh escaped through Casey's pursed lips one more time. "Okay, I'll do it, but you're paying for the membership."

Mica gave a fist pump. "Yay! What's the worst thing that could happen?"

"Worse thing to happen is that I have one bad date. We'll never win the vacation. We are the two unluckiest people I've ever known."

"Come on. Let's go back to your house and get on the computer. We can sign on to the website and get the application we need to complete.

Two hours later, they were on the tenth and final page of the application and questionnaire.

"What color would you say my hair is?" Mica tipped her head forward trying to see her bangs. "And don't say mixed grey. I can always pull out the grey ones."

"In that case I'd have to answer bald.*"*

"Very funny."

"I guess I'd say honey blonde." Casey's brown eyes met Mica's green ones. "If you had to describe me in three words, what would they be?"

"Wait, what number are you on?"

Casey leaned forward and squinted at the laptop screen. "I think it says thirty-eight." She turned the screen around and pointed to the question.

"Thirty-six. You need your computer glasses."

"They're on the table over there. These are fine."

Mica leaned over, got the glasses, and handed them to her friend.

"Here. You know you'll have a headache if you keep going with your regular readers."

"Thanks. I need your three words."

"Well, lazy comes to mind first. No, maybe stubborn. Or…"

"I'm going to kill you, Mica." Casey did her best to hide her smile. "Because you're making me do this, the least you can do is help me."

"I did help you, I gave you your glasses. How many times do I have to hear that complaint?"

"You'll be hearing it until one of us wins that vacation. Come on. I don't know what to answer."

Mica buried her toes under Casey's thigh. "My feet are cold. Don't you have any heat in this place?"

Ignoring Mica's distraction, Casey asked again. "Three words…specifically, 'If your best friend were to describe your personality, what three words would she use?' Since the objective is to get someone to choose me as a date, please try to make them positive words."

"Okay." Mica tipped her head to the side and rested her cheek on her palm. "I guess I'd say loving, loyal, and genuine."

"Really?"

"Yeah. What words would you pick for me?"

Casey thoughtfully tapped her chin with her index finger. "Loyal, loving, and sexy."

Mica's head snapped up. "Sexy? Really? *You* think *I'm* sexy?"

"Of course I do. You turn heads wherever you go. Probably your most endearing quality is that you're totally oblivious to the looks you get."

"How come I didn't know that?" Mica's eyebrows knit together, arching upward to nearly touch in the middle of her forehead.

"I would guess it's because you've never made me complete a questionnaire that required a million responses before. You especially have sexy eyebrows." Casey put on her glasses and began typing.

Mica shrugged. "Humph. Sexy. Who knew?"

Finally finished, they each printed out a copy of their questionnaire and compared their answers. Casey laughed and pointed to the top of the form. "With few exceptions, we could have filled in one form and just changed the names and addresses at the top. God, we're like two peas in a pod."

CHAPTER THREE

CASEY HARRISON GLANCED AT her watch for what must have been the thirty-sixth time in the last hour. She covered her mouth with her hand, attempting to stifle the stubborn yawn that begged to escape her clenched lips. Making an ultimate effort, she relaxed her facial muscles and forced herself to keep one ear tuned to the incessant chatter. Words cascaded from her companion with the same speed and volume that water gushed over Niagara Falls.

It seemed like forever that she'd been waiting for her Match Me date to finish the remainder of her half-eaten dessert. If she'd just shut up for a few seconds, she might finish those last few bites of key lime pie and we could get out of here. *I wonder if mind control is a real super power. Do I have it? What the hell, I'll give it a go.* Closing out the background noise, she squinted her eyes and beamed her wishes toward her date.

"Blah, blah, blah…"

Oh God…was that a question? Casey's senses flashed into high alert, trying to recall the last words her date had uttered. Her brain shifted into overdrive, frantically searching for conversational details. Her heart fluttered as she hoped she'd not been caught with her mind adrift. An audible exhale escaped her lips when the woman smiled. Nell's fork, containing a tiny sample of the sweet, made the journey half way toward Casey. "Do you want some of this pie?"

"No, thanks. I'm stuffed." Casey forced herself to watch her date swivel the dessert plate around and take another infinitesimal forkful of pie. She moved the morsel delicately toward her mouth, then chewed it exactly fourteen times before washing away any remnants with the last drop of her coffee.

How can anyone chew key lime pie fourteen times? Casey groaned inwardly when her date, Cornelia, signaled for the server to refill her coffee cup. *Cornelia. What parent in their right mind would saddle this young woman with an old-fashioned name like that? Ah! There's a question to ask.*

As the server refilled the coffee for her date, Casey declined more beverage and asked for the check. "So, Cornelia...that's an unusual name. How did your parents come up with that?"

Cornelia stirred four teaspoons of sugar and a generous amount of cream into her coffee. "Oh, I get that question a lot. I was named after my mother's grandmother. I hated my name when I was a kid, because my classmates tagged me with the nickname Corny."

Casey felt a momentary pang of sorrow for the little girl Corny once was.

"Once I got old enough, I started introducing myself as Nell. That's what I prefer. Unfortunately, I had to put my full name on the application for the dating service questionnaire."

Casey tensed, hoping nobody heard that last comment. She still felt a bit embarrassed that she'd allowed Mica to convince her to participate in the computer-matched dating experiment.

Nell was still droning on about her name. "So, I decided to look up the meaning of my name. Its origin is Irish, meaning strong willed or wise. I also found that it is sometimes used as a translation of Conchubbar. Did you know that his name can be translated as Connor of the Red Eyebrows?"

Casey shook her head and wondered if her eyes had yet glazed over.

"Well, he is well-known as an Irish chieftain who reportedly had more than one pupil in each eye. Fortunately, I didn't inherit that trait." Nell giggled at her own humor. "The other meaning of his name is High Desire." Nell batted her eyes.

"Really?" Casey hoped that the groan she heard inside her head was, in fact, inaudible. "I have to admit that is information I didn't know." Hoping to discourage any follow-up to the flirtation, Casey once again glanced at her watch.

Obviously oblivious to Casey's subliminal message, Nell asked, "How did you come to be called Casey?"

"My dad's favorite poem was 'Casey at the Bat.'"

"What's that? I don't think I've ever heard of it." Nell scraped off another sliver of pie and began her chewing ritual.

Yet again, Casey regretted allowing Mica to convince her to try computer dating. She forced herself not to count and tried to focus on her answer.

"Casey?"

"Oh, sorry. I was trying to remember who wrote the poem.

Anyway, it was written in the late 1800s about a baseball player named Casey, who struck out at bat and brought no joy to the fictitious town of Mudville."

"Oh." Nell reached for the last bite of pie and silence fell between the women.

A smile darted across Casey's lips. *I'm fourteen chews away from near freedom.* She picked up the check and pulled her credit card from her pocket.

"I guess you're ready to leave. What's my share?"

"Please, my treat."

"That's very nice of you. I'll pay next time."

Would that we live so long. Casey bit her bottom lip and leaned forward. "I'm sorry, Nell. You're obviously a lovely young woman with a lot to offer the right person. I don't think the computer got it right in our case. We are complete opposites with nothing in common."

"I've heard opposites attract. Obviously, you don't believe that."

"Uh, no. I don't believe that. I marvel that this computer dating thing got us so wrong." Casey caught the server's eye and handed her the check and credit card as she approached.

"What's so wrong about this match?"

"First, I'm forty-two and you're not yet thirty. We have yet to find one interest we have in common. We have different tastes in music, films, and hobbies. As you would say, that's an 'L' as opposed to a 'W,' meaning win. Half the time, I don't understand what the hell you're talking about. I'm v witty and p smart. Why not just say very and pretty? Does it take that much effort to add a second syllable or finish a word? Then, there's the last straw...you don't like Rachel Maddow, and you can watch Fox News without becoming ill. Lord save me."

"Oh, I thought we were starting to warm up to each other a bit by the end of dessert." Nell shrugged. "I guess you're right. You forgot that I can't live without coffee and you only drink tea." Nell cocked her head and her eyes narrowed. "Since we're being brutally honest, you're kind of androgynous. I like more feminine women, like myself. You're sort of a sporty lesbian."

A furrow appeared between Casey's brows, as she glanced down at her purse and the heels she was wearing for her date. *I guess I'm not exactly a femme, but it's not like I wore cleats.*

"Oh, and you're way too tall for me. Plus, I prefer shoulder length or longer blonde hair and green eyes. Your eyes and hair are dark, and it's cut way too short for my tastes. As for the Democrat and Republican thing, I merely said I'm not overly fond of Rachel. I only watch the other channel to be prepared for what they'll try to pull next." She propped her chin on her palm. "I think this Match Me company is a little weird. It's like they matched the opposite of everything I asked for. Besides everything we've already mentioned, you're way too quiet for me."

Casey arched her eyebrow, gave in to her sense of better judgement, and swallowed her snarky retort. She opted not to mention that she couldn't have squeezed a word into the conversation with a sledge hammer and a full can of lubricant. "Well, there's one thing we agree on then. I'll also admit that this is the most interesting conversation we've had all night." The server returned with a brown leather check holder containing Casey's credit card and the receipt to sign.

As Casey started to add the tip to the total, Nell reached over and stopped her. "Please, at least let me get the tip."

"Okay, thanks."

Nell pushed a generous tip across the table. Casey took her copy, signed the credit card receipt, and placed it in the leather folder along with the cash for the server. She set the pen on top and looked up to meet Nell's eyes. "What made you get involved in computer dating? Obviously, we're not a good match. However, you're really very nice, and certainly attractive."

"Well, thank you. You're cute too, especially when you smile. You have perfect teeth and great dimples. I like the way your lips turn up at the corners and how expressive your eyes are." Nell sighed and quickly changed the topic back to herself. "To answer your question, I guess I'm tired of going to bars. It seems like all my squad, uh, I mean friends, are hooked up or married. Although they still invite me to join them, I feel extra. I want someone of my own, and it appears I'm not going to wake up one morning and find her in bed next to me without trying something different to find her. The same old, same old doesn't seem to work, so I gave computer dating a try." Nell giggled. "What about you? Obviously, the love of your life was already spoken for or didn't sign up for Match Me."

"Love of my life?"

"Yeah. You're here doing a Match Me date and got me."

Casey allowed herself to smile. "Oh, I see. I guess you have a point."

Nell shrugged. "You were my only match, you know."

"And you were mine. Maybe there's a shortage of lesbians."

They joined each other in laughter for the first time that evening.

Nell picked the napkin, folded it, and placed it on the table. "I think you might be onto something there. They're a new company. Maybe not enough of us signed up and they had to make matches from the limited pool they had."

"Sad to think we were the best match they could make for either of us. It was like they saw lesbian and said...there you go, done." Again, they laughed. Casey smiled at her companion. "I admit that earlier I was confounded. However, I can't say it's a complete loss. You're quite a lovely young woman, or should I say, you're a v-lovely young woman?"

"See, you can speak my English."

Casey winked. "That's debatable. Friends?"

"Sure. Maybe we should keep the computer dating thing on the down low...uh, between us."

"At least I've heard that expression before, so I'm not a complete dinosaur."

In silent agreement, the women walked to the corner. Casey scanned the street. "Is your car close by?"

"I took an Uber."

"Let me give you a lift home." Casey led the way to her car. She closed the door behind Nell and walked around to the other side and buckled herself into the driver's seat. "I'd like you to meet my friend, Mica. Maybe we can find a movie or some activity to do. She's the same age as me, so you'll have to continue translating for us both. I'm sure we can have fun though. Mica and I aren't a couple, so you won't feel extra. None of us will."

Casey stopped the car in front of Nell's apartment and opened the door for her date.

"You didn't have to do that. I could have gotten out on my own, especially now that our date is over. I don't expect my friends to do things like that for me." Nell stood on her tiptoes and pulled Casey down for a kiss on the cheek. "Thank you. I know it wasn't a great date until the end, when we really started to communicate. I'm sorry if I talked too much. I talk a lot when I'm nervous. I had such high hopes for tonight."

"All is not lost. We each made a new friend tonight."

"Agreed."

Casey paused at her car and shook her head. "I can't believe I'm going to do this, because I personally swore off blind dates years ago. However, there's a very nice young woman at work that you might get along with. Would you be willing to meet her if I can arrange it?"

"Rad. Worst case, she's another new friend, right? Maybe we can all chill together the first time?"

"Okay, I'll ask my friend Mica if she'd be willing to come with us.'" Casey winked. "I'll call you. Goodnight, Corny."

"Hey, Slugger. Knock off that crap!"

"Deal." Casey was still smiling when she pulled away. The final memory of her date was Nell waving in the rearview mirror.

CHAPTER FOUR

CASEY PULLED INTO HER driveway and chuckled because her living room lights were on. She'd have bet her life savings that Mica would be anxious to hear about the date.

Mica swept the door open, filling its frame. "How was it?"

"Rad."

"What? Bad?"

"Well that too, although what I said was rad with an r, not bad with a b." Casey smiled at Mica's quizzical expression. She climbed the two steps to her front door and placed her hand in the middle of Mica's chest. "Come on, let me in."

Mica stepped back to allow Casey entrance. "Hm. Judging from your expression, I'd guess you didn't make a love match."

"Not exactly. She was actually quite sweet the last half hour or so we were together, despite the agony of the first two hours." Casey grasped Mica's forearms and backed her up. Turning away, she closed the door before following Mica down the hallway into the living room.

"Drink?" Mica raised her nearly empty glass.

"Sure. What are you having?"

"Vodka and orange juice."

Casey nodded. "Sounds perfect. Throw a splash of Galliano in there too." Casey had learned to love a well-made Harvey Wallbanger because of Grams. It was her grandmother's drink of choice. "I'm going to go change while you mix the drinks."

Only minutes later, dressed more comfortably, Casey stopped in the hallway to watch her friend who had settled on the sofa with Simon. A smile played on her lips, as she observed Mica kiss the top of his black head and then scratch the white tuxedo marking on his chest. She waved her hand to free the cat hair from her fingers, before she brushed evidence of his visit from her pants. "God, Simon, why aren't you bald? I have more of your hair on me than you do."

Obviously, they had been curled up together on the sofa before Casey returned home. Mica stretched out her back and brushed her hair away from her face. Her honey-brown hair was still sun streaked from the time they'd spent at the beach during the summer.

"Pfff." Mica tried to clear the cat hair from her face. "Simon, you need a good brushing. I'll have to have a chat with your mother about that when she gets back out here." Mica glanced up, her pale-green eyes sparkling in the glow of the table lamp. "What?"

"Nothing," Casey replied, a soft smile on her face. As she approached her friend, she noted the few extra pounds Mica had added over the years, making her almost curvy. The wisps of grey hair were hardly noticeable, blended in among the sun's highlights. "I was just thinking how about how we've been friends for so long that I don't know what I'd do without you."

Mica approached. "Nor I you." She wrapped her arms around Casey and gave her a quick hug and a kiss on the cheek. She leaned back and brushed her hand against Casey's cheek before tapping her nose with her index finger. "Come on, you. I want to hear about your date."

They settled with the end table between them, Mica on the sofa where she'd been sitting, and Casey choosing the rocker. They clinked glasses before each took a sip of her drink. Casey was grateful for the friend who knew her all too well and gave her time to gather her thoughts.

"Match Me protocols don't allow person-to-person contact before the date. The limited assumptions I did form had little correlation to reality. First, if my birth date was a scant three years earlier, I could have been this woman's mother."

"Oh my. Did you find anything to talk about? What does she do?"

"Nell's definitely bright. Even though she hasn't been working that long, she's already an office manager. She's cute as a button, and only about two-thirds my height."

Casey tugged at the top of both ears.

"What are you doing?"

"Just checking to be sure she didn't talk one of my ears off." Casey chuckled. "Poor kid admitted she talks more when she's nervous."

"Oh, now I feel sorry for her. Were you nice?"

"Mostly. I was bored to tears most of the evening. I hope I didn't show it too obviously." Casey swirled the ice cubes in her drink before taking a sip. "Umm, good, thank you." She set her glass on the table and leaned her cheek on her palm. "The poor kid really tried, I guess. I didn't recognize the name of a single song she claimed as her favorite. When did we get this old?"

"What do you mean, *we*?"

"Get over it...we're the same age." Casey glared at her friend until she got the effect she loved.

Mica's eyebrows arched and tried to reach for each other. "I know what you mean. The kids at work talk about going to concerts all the time, drooling over people that, for the most part, I've never heard of. One of them just went to see an artist who made all the rest of the band members wear some sort of disguise, so only he was recognized. Then there's that performer who wears a wig that covers her whole face. I admit it, I just don't get it."

"My point precisely. I won't even delve into our discussion about politics. Can you imagine a lesbian who doesn't watch Rachel? She watches Fox News."

"No!" Mica's hand flew to her mouth.

"She admitted that she really doesn't support their views. She likes a couple of the reporters on there who she says are fairer than others. She's a better woman than I am. I can't bring myself to watch them." Casey took another drink. "For the first ninety percent of the date, I couldn't wait to get out of there. She chews her food precisely fourteen times. I swear I could feel my hair turning grey and the calcium leaving my bones, as I sat there waiting for her to finish."

Mica's laugh garnered a dirty look in response. "So, if that's the first ninety percent, what happened at the end that made it better?"

"I don't know. She was quite nice, despite how little we had in common and how old I felt. She used expressions I've never heard. Once she realized I wouldn't be asking for another date, she seemed to relax, and we began to actually talk to each other." Casey snickered. "Maybe we need some younger friends. I'm not ready to grow old just yet. I was thinking of setting her up with Trish."

"Trish? From work?"

"Yes. She's single, smart, and maybe only five or six years older than Nell."

"Oh, interesting idea."

"Glad you think so. I volunteered you to go along with us."

"Swell." Mica rolled her eyes.

"Are you being disingenuous?"

Mica shrugged. "Only a little. I'm sure we'll have fun. We always do. We'll just introduce them and sit back and watch the fun. Let's go bowling. We haven't done that for a while, and it's a good first date."

"Speaking of dates, tomorrow night is your first Match Me date.

Where are you going?"

"Romano's. We're meeting there at seven." Mica stood up. "I'd better get going. What are you doing tomorrow?"

"I think I'll give Trish a call and see if she's open to having lunch. Then I'll break the news about her potential new squeeze."

"Optimist." Mica scratched Simon behind the ear. "Goodbye, buddy. I enjoyed our cuddle." She leaned over and kissed Casey on top of the head. "You going to visit your grandmother tomorrow?"

"Yup, before lunch. I worry about her being alone in that old house. Want to come?"

"Sure. I'll collect you around nine? We can stop and pick up some of those blueberry muffins she likes from the market."

Casey reached out and squeezed Mica's hand. "Thanks. See you in the morning." At the door, they embraced. As Mica walked to her car, Casey called out, "Phone me when you get home."

Mica wiggled her fingers over her shoulder in acknowledgment.

CHAPTER FIVE

"I'M HERE, OUT FRONT. I have a muffin for you from Bucky's. Don't make me wait too long, or I'll take a bite of it."

"You're a lifesaver, Mica. I'm running late and didn't have time for breakfast. Be right out." Casey was still on the phone as she closed and locked her front door. "Morning."

"Buckle in and I'll give you the muffin."

"Hey! There's a bite missing. I didn't keep you waiting." Casey's attempted pout turned into a warm chuckle. She took the offered muffin. "Want another bite before we get under way?"

"No, I'm good. I already ate mine. I just did that to ruffle your feathers. You're so easy that way." Mica pulled away from the curb and headed for Grams' house.

"I was hungry and stopped at the market to get one for each of us and Grams' favorites for her. Does she know we're coming?"

"Yes, I called her last night."

Casey's grandmother lived in a huge, old Victorian on a large plot of land at the edge of the town. The large green structure was the house she was born in and had lived in all her life. Casey's mother had grown up there as well, and Casey had played in the multistoried structure. The attic had been an endless source of entertainment on rainy days during her younger years. Her mind drifted to the times she'd spent with Grams, recalling her grandmother's endless good humor and ready smile. Lately, that sharp wit and ready smile were much less frequent. Now nearly ninety-two, Grams' health was starting to betray her. At times, age-related aches and pains made her just short of cranky. Although arthritis curled her once dexterous fingers, it didn't slow her production on any number of her crafts.

In less than twenty minutes, the two women had arrived at their destination and parked the car in the driveway. They cut across the well-manicured lawn to reach the entryway. Casey pushed the doorbell and was rewarded with a typical Grams' greeting.

"You took your sweet time getting here, girls. This old woman could have starved to death waiting on you two."

Knowing it was useless to argue, they fell in line. Grams offered her wrinkled cheek for the requisite kiss and reached for the bag of muffins Mica extended toward her. "Get on in here. I've made tea."

Grams walked quickly down the hallway ahead of them. Casey would have recognized the sound of Grams' quick-stepped stride almost anywhere. Always chilly, she wore a sweatshirt over her turtleneck, and matching warmup pants. Grams was as spunky as the bright-red cardinal on her shirt.

They followed the tiny, older woman into the kitchen. Entering there was like passing through a portal into the forties. An intricate, charcoal-grey border pattern established the boundary of the black and white tile floor. The green-tiled walls were accented by black baseboards, drawer pulls, and hinges. Glass inserts in the white cabinet doors displayed the decorative grapevines of the dinnerware. The white appliances were the only modernization the kitchen had seen since Gramps renovated the house when he returned from the war.

The kitchen table was already set, and cups with tea bags awaited the hot water she had heating on the stove.

"Let me get that, Grams. Have a seat and get yourself a muffin." Mica went to fetch the water from the stove.

Grams opened the bag and placed the sweets on a plate. She split one open and prepared her feast. Her first bite left tooth marks in the butter she'd slathered on the muffin and brought a grin to her face. "What are you two up to?"

"Mostly just chores." Casey answered for both.

"You must be busy." Grams glared in Casey's direction. "You haven't been around much."

"I was just here two days ago. I do have to work, you know."

"Well, let me get my violin."

Used to her grandmother's constant complaints, Casey countered the accusation. "I know, you think I don't come enough. If you had your way, you'd have me here every day. Next you'll be telling me that I'll miss you when you're gone." It was a phrase Casey heard at least once per visit.

"Nope. I won't. I've changed my mind. I'm not going."

Casey reached over and squeezed her wrinkled hand. "Well, some good news for a change."

"Seriously, Casey. You should sell your place and move in upstairs. You wouldn't even know I was here, and think about all that money you'd save."

"You know I can't do that. You're allergic to Simon. You'd be sneezing and coughing twenty-four hours a day. I'd get no sleep, causing me to eventually lose my job. You'd have to support me. Quickly, you'd grow tired of that and throw me out. I'd be homeless, have to turn to prostitution, and you'd no longer be able to brag about me to all your friends."

"Bull cocky. What a load of manure that was." Grams swatted away the words as a chuckle escaped. "What makes you think I brag about you anyway?"

Casey pointed in the direction of the house next door. "Mrs. Johnson told me she gets sick of hearing about your granddaughter."

"She's a meddlesome old bat. She shouldn't tell you what we talk about." Grams took another bite of her muffin. "These are pretty good. They still can't hold a candle to my 'magic bullets.'"

Grams was famous for her creation throughout the neighborhood. Homemade oatmeal muffins with bran, diced prunes, chopped apricots, and walnut pieces were the magic bullets Grams swore kept her regular. She always had at least a dozen in the freezer. Several neighbors were converts and would stop by for a couple to 'set them free' when they developed a problem.

"What do you think, Grams?" Mica teased. "Let's go into business together. You make the muffins, and I'll peddle them door to door. We could make a fortune."

"I'm game, if you are." Grams always laughed at Mica's lighthearted teasing. "You girls need to visit more often and stay longer."

The girls had stayed for an hour and a half. Before they left, Grams showed them the latest pair of roly-poly slippers she was crocheting. On the way out, Casey stopped to admire her favorite quilling pieces, proudly displayed in frames on the hall wall. "I love this one, especially, Grams."

"It's in the will."

"Stop. You just told me you're not going. That suits me just fine." She wrapped her arms around the tiny woman and gave a gentle squeeze. "I'll see you in a couple of days. Call me if you need anything." Casey and Mica left Grams standing in the doorway and headed for their car. Grams gave them a wave and a smile before she closed the door.

Buckling her seat belt, Casey sighed. "I always feel so sad when I leave her. I know she's lonely rattling around in that big house all alone. She finally allowed me to hire someone to do the yard a couple of years ago. Last year, she gave in and allowed me to hire Hannah to clean, but Grams still cleans the house the day before Hannah comes. The two of them sit and giggle like school girls for the time the woman is supposed to be cleaning. Hannah was concerned I'd be mad. Grams gets more from the visits than cleaning, and it appears to be what she needs, so it's okay. We ended up arranging that Hannah cleans as much as she can while she's here on regular days. Once or twice a month, I let Hannah know when I'm taking Grams out for her hair appointment and mani-pedi. Hannah hires a friend, and they whip through and do a thorough cleaning of the place. It seems to work for everyone."

"Have you thought about moving in with her?"

"Grams only started suggesting that over the past few months. Most of the time, she makes noises like she resents me meddling in her life. It almost killed her when she started having trouble paying her bills on her own and couldn't balance her checkbook. She used to be able to calculate in her mind faster than I could using a calculator. Suddenly, it became an impossible task. I got around that by saying it would be fun if we paid our bills together. I showed her how I pay bills online. She was amazed that they don't charge for that service and was impressed she could pay bills without buying stamps. They kept all the records she needed. All we had to do was keep track of what checks she wrote, and we could see when they were cashed online. It works great. She only has about three or four bills a month."

"You've been very good to her since your mom passed. She's lucky to have you."

Tears filled Casey's eyes. "I'm lucky to still have her, especially with Dad and Mom both gone. It's sad to see Grams growing older. She is an amazing woman...well ahead of her time. My grandmother has worked all her life, long before it was socially acceptable for a woman to do so. She was married three times and divorced twice. My mother told me Grams complained that her last husband wasn't romantic enough for her."

"Whoa! Go Grams!" Mica squinted in recollection. "He's the one I knew, right?. He was a funny guy."

Casey nodded. "He was. No matter how much she complained about him, she still misses him."

The pair grew quiet, as they drove toward Casey's home. As Mica pulled up, she asked Casey to stop over before she left for her date. "I'd like you to check out my outfit."

"Sure. I can fill you in on what Trish says, too." Casey got out of the car. "I'll see you later." Mica grinned and waited for Casey to close the door before she pulled away.

AJ Adaire

CHAPTER SIX

"I'M HERE." CASEY STUCK her head inside Mica's front door. Where are you?"

"Here, in the bedroom. Come on up."

Casey climbed the stairs and made her way down the hall to Mica's bedroom. She took a moment to admire Mica, who was standing in her underwear in front of her bed, staring at half of her wardrobe strewn in front of her. "If that's what you're wearing, I'm sure she'll think you're hot." Casey pursed her lips and cocked an eyebrow. "Maybe just a touch of lipstick…"

"Stop. You're the one who wears darker lipstick. It goes better with your skin tone. I'm a gloss or lip balm gal all the way. I prefer the more natural look."

Casey shrugged one shoulder. "A touch of color would look nice on your lips. You're lucky though, you've got those gorgeous, green eyes and dark lashes. You barely need a touch of mascara."

Mica ignored the compliment and continued to obsess about an outfit. She discarded yet another top onto the pile. "Come on, help me. I can't decide what to wear. It seems like a millennium since I had a date. I want to be casual and comfy, yet stylish."

Casey picked out a pair of well-cut trousers and a soft, pale-green shirt. "This is my favorite outfit of yours. It brings out the green in your eyes and shows off your curves."

"Ha! Curves. I'm getting fat. Curves is a polite way to tell me that." Mica tilted her head and pressed her lips together as she examined the outfit.

"No, not fat. I'm giving you my honest opinion." Casey allowed her eyes to again travel the length of Mica's body before she walked over and sat in the chair near the window.

"Okay, you know I trust you. Green it is. Tell me about your meeting with Trish, while I hang up all this stuff." Mica slipped her robe on and tied the belt loosely around her waist.

"We had a nice time. At first, she wasn't too interested in my idea.

She told me she swore off blind dates in her teens. As we talked, and I told her we'd go with them, she gave in and said she'd give it a go. We're all set for next Saturday, so don't make plans to follow up tonight's hot date next weekend."

"I wish I hadn't signed up for Match Me. I'm not looking forward to doing this."

"Why don't you take your shower and get dressed?" Casey stood and moved toward the doorway. "I'll go make us a drink, and we'll relax for a little while before you have to leave."

Half an hour later, Mica came down the stairway and walked toward the drink Casey held extended. "You look beautiful, Mica."

Mica's eyes met Casey's as if searching for any signs of insincerity.

"I mean it. Come on, sit down and relax for a few minutes."

Glancing at her watch, Mica asked, "Why can't I just call her off and the two of us go out like usual?"

"Don't forget, this whole Match Me caper was your idea. You're the one in search of romance."

Mica shook her head. "No, I said I was interested in an all-expense-paid vacation. I clearly don't remember mentioning that I was seeking romance." The two women finished their drinks, enjoying conversation as relaxed and comfortable as a well-worn pair of jeans.

"It's time." Mica's watch chimed, notifying her of her scheduled departure time. "I'll call you when I get in."

***

Mica was seated against the wall watching for her date, when a casually dressed customer entered and spoke briefly with the hostess. The trim, well-toned woman made eye contact with Mica, as the hostess led her toward the table. Mica stood up to greet her companion as she neared the table, noting that she stood slightly taller than her date's five foot six.

"Hello." Extending her hand, she said, "I'm Lisa Taft."

"Mica Baxter." She took the cool hand into her own. "It's nice to meet you."

Lisa's mauve colored lips curled upward and parted to reveal white, even teeth. "The pleasure is all mine." Lisa sat the handbag that matched her shoes on the chair next to her.

Mica completed her appraisal, noting the flattering, jaw-length salt and pepper hair, as she waited for Lisa to speak.

"Do you want a cocktail or some wine?"

Mica nodded. "I had a rye and ginger ale with a friend of mine before I left home. Maybe I'll have another of those."

The woman who approached was the same one who had seated them. "Good evening, and welcome to Romano's. Thank you for joining us this evening. I'm the owner, Theresa Romano."

"Hello," Lisa and Mica responded simultaneously.

"We had a server involved in a car accident this evening, so I'm doing double duty tonight. I'll be taking your drink order to help a bit. Please, be patient with your server. She's taken on some additional tables, and we're a little busy right now. Serena will be over as soon as she's available. In the meantime, enjoy some of this." She placed a basket, full of crisp, homemade Italian bread, and a bottle of deep, rich olive oil on the table.

Lisa smiled. "Tell her not to worry, please. We're in no hurry, so she can take her time. I hope your employee will be okay."

"Thank you for your concern. May I take your drink order?"

Nodding in Mica's direction, Lisa replied, "She'll have a rye and ginger ale and I'll have an iced San Pellegrino, please." As the owner left to deal with the drinks, Lisa asked, "What do you do for a living?"

"I'm a physical therapist. I'm part owner in a physical therapy office/gym called Fit As A Fiddle. In addition to providing physical therapy, our business is geared to older clientele more interested in maintaining a healthy level of physical fitness than building massive muscles. How about you?"

"Nutritionist." Lisa turned her attention to the menu.

Inwardly, Mica groaned. She'd been eyeing the spaghetti carbonara.

Their server hurried over with their drinks. "Hello, I'm Serena. I'm sorry to keep you waiting." She set Mica's cocktail in front of her, then opened and poured Lisa's San Pellegrino. "Are you ready to order?"

Lisa tapped her lip with a painted nail, as she checked the open menu in front of her on the table. She pointed to her choice. "I'll have the grilled salmon. Instead of the potato, I'd like a salad with the dressing on the side."

"And for you?"

Mica looked up and sighed, "Grilled chicken and a salad as well, please."

"Got it." Serena smiled and turned toward the kitchen.

"You made a healthy choice." Lisa studied Mica with a steely, hazel-eyed gaze. Slowly, a knowing smile appeared. "That isn't what you wanted to order, is it?"

Mica dropped her eyes. Only a few seconds elapsed before she straightened her spine and sat up taller. "No. Given my druthers, I'd have had the carbonara."

"Why didn't you get that?"

Mica shrugged. "You're a nutritionist. I guess I wanted to impress you."

"You're honest. I like that." Lisa leaned forward. "However, please don't do that again for me. I'm not your mother. Life is too short to give up on your own needs and wants. Although not the greatest of choices, carbonara won't kill you if you don't make a habit of it and do some exercise to make up for the transgression." She replaced her previous expression with a warm smile. "Over the years, I've learned that if my clients continually deprive themselves of food choices they would naturally make, they eventually fall completely off the wagon and don't succeed in keeping their weight under control. It's all about balance. I made the choice to eat wisely for my main course, in hopes you'd split a dessert with me. I've heard their desserts are to die for."

"Now you're talking." Mica shared laughter with her chuckling companion. "I'm almost sure I can choke down the plain, grilled chicken, if I know I have a treat coming later."

Conversation was easy. The topic of the restaurant's reputation for exceptional Italian food and homemade desserts was quickly exhausted, and Lisa turned their discourse to Match Me, specifically, and computer dating in general. Lisa seemed to hesitate before she asked the next question. "I hope you won't think this too personal...I'm fifty-six. I tend to date women my age or slightly older. I requested a match in the mid-fifties to mid-sixties range and, if you fall into that category, I want to know who your beautician is."

"I'll be forty-two next month."

The arrival of their meals slowed their sharing of information until all the food was served and Serena had returned to the kitchen. Lisa put a scant teaspoon of dressing on her salad. She cut the tomato slice into small pieces and delicately dipped the tip of one of them into the dressing and placed it into her mouth. "Have you had many responses to your submission to Match Me?"

"No. You were my only match."

"I got two names. I'm curious. Was I what you expected or requested?" Lisa waited patiently, as Mica considered her response.

28

"I'm not sure I had expectations. I hope you won't be offended or think I wasted your time if I confess something to you?"

Lisa nodded. "Not at all."

"I mostly did this to get my name in the drawing for a free vacation and fulfill the requirements of the contest. If I met someone I clicked with, I'd consider it a bonus. I've done computer dating before, and frankly didn't hold out much hope to meet anyone. I'm comfortable with my current life."

Lisa's eye's narrowed. "Wife? You already have a partner?"

"What? No, not wife...*life*. I'm definitely single."

"Sorry, I thought you said wife." Lisa chuckled at the misunderstanding. "It's a little noisy in here."

Mica placed her knife and fork on her plate and wiped her mouth with her napkin. "I didn't intend to get into this serious a conversation tonight. You're easy to be with...easy to talk to."

"Is that a good or a bad thing?"

"Definitely good."

Lisa finished the last bite of her meal. "Who is it then, or what makes you so settled and happy?"

"I'm in a good place. My business partner and I have been spending a lot of time together lately. We get along well, laugh a lot, and mostly like similar things."

"And you're in love with her?"

Mica blinked. It was the first time she had ever considered that as a serious possibility. "Hmm." Buying time as she considered her response, Mica took a sip of her cocktail. "That's not a possibility I've ever entertained. We've been friends for a long time. We've known each other since high school. She already knew she was gay. Despite having a nagging doubt about myself even back then, probably since grade school, I was doing my best to prove my theory wrong. Once we got into grad school, my guy du jour and I used to double date with her and her girlfriend of the moment. It took me a while longer to figure myself out."

"You never considered, you know, with her?"

"Never seriously. I couldn't stand it if I lost her friendship. You see, she has this thing..."

"Thing?" Lisa paused with her glass halfway to her lips.

"Yeah. There was a bad break-up in college. I don't want to say too much. It's a personal and sensitive subject for her. She told me the story a long time ago, and rarely even talks about it with me anymore. Usually the most she'll say is, 'I could never be involved with a friend, because I learned that lesson the hard way.' She is so adamant when she says it, there's no doubt she means it."

"And there's no way to change her mind?"

"The point was moot, because Casey was my friend by the time I came out, and I loved her as such. Funny, in all these years we've never been single at the same time, until now. We parted ways with our respective girlfriends about ten months ago. We naturally grew closer and helped each other fill the void left by our absent partners."

The server's assistant approached and cleared the table. Shortly thereafter, Serena returned for their dessert order. "Ms. Romano said that dessert is on her because you've been so patient and understanding."

"There's certainly no need," Lisa said. "Please let her know we appreciate her kindness."

They ordered a tiramisu and two forks. "The serving is large. I'll split it for you." Serena winked at Lisa. It seemed like only an instant later that the rich dessert appeared. Lisa ordered a coffee and Mica asked for tea.

"Okay, where were we?" Lisa broke off a piece of the sweet with her fork. "Oh yes, your business partner that you love." Her left eyebrow did a little wiggle above eyes that twinkled with mischief. "Have you thought of taking your relationship to the next level?"

"Not seriously, although, who wouldn't want Casey as a lover? She's perfect."

Lisa smiled. "You're obviously smitten."

"I would never endanger our friendship. She's made her position clear. If I were to force the issue and ask for more, I believe it would cost our friendship." Mica grew quiet. "I don't think I could live without her in my life. She says that friends-to-lovers relationships end in the loss of everything. So, friends it is."

"I can tell you that is not always the case. I lost my lover of thirty-four years to cancer, a little over two years ago. We met in college and became friends. One night, we went to a party and had more to drink than normal. Drunken confessions turned into drunken love making." Lisa's eyes drifted and clouded in recall. Almost as if talking to herself, she told Mica how they couldn't look each other in the eyes the next morning. "I slunk out of bed and went to shower. I was just stepping into the stall, when Susan opened the door and said, 'Let's not do this to each other. Be honest. You love me, don't you?' I didn't even answer her, just pulled her into my arms and kissed her with my entire heart and soul."

"What would have happened if she hadn't been brave enough to say something?"

"Who can say? I'm reasonably certain that we'd have worked it out eventually. I know there was no one else in the world that was right for me." Lisa's eyes brimmed and she looked away. A few seconds passed before she took a deep breath and blinked away her tears. "Look at us. What a pair. Neither of us should really be here. Both of us are in love with somebody else."

"Wait a minute...I never said I was *in love* with my partner."

"Right. Okay. I'm still in love with my gal, and you are here only because you want to win a contest. Is that better?"

"I can live with that statement." Mica chuckled. She caught Serena's eye and tapped her cup to indicate she wanted a refill. "Shall we talk about less serious matters?"

"Sure. How about this weather?"

"What?"

"As you suggested, a less serious topic." Lisa added some milk to her coffee, while Mica added sugar to her tea. "Think about it, people can always talk about the weather.

Mica tilted her head to the side and shrugged. Placing her spoon on her saucer she took a sip of her tea.

"I had a friend, Edward. His business phone message gave all the requisite information and he ended it with, 'Hey, how about this weather!' It always made me smile. It's one of those phrases that fits all occasions. Wind, snow, sun, the perfect day...no matter what, that phrase works."

"I guess it does." Shaking her head, Mica rewarded Lisa's efforts with a hearty laugh.

They talked a little longer before splitting the check and leaving Serena a generous tip. After bidding the owner a good evening, the two women stood in front of the restaurant to say their farewell with a brief hug. "Thank you for a wonderful evening, Mica. One of the things I miss most without Susan is good company over a meal. I enjoyed our conversation. We've talked about where each of us is in life, and it appears that neither of us is ready to move forward into any sort of serious relationship. Thank you for helping me to figure that out tonight. As much as I thought I was ready, I know I'm not. I hope we can see each other again as friends."

"I'd like that, too." They exchanged contact information and left in their separate directions.

***

Casey picked up on the first ring of her phone. "Are you home, Mica?"

"No, I'm in the car. I'll be home in a few minutes."

"How was your date?"

"It was nice. She's a lovely woman. I liked her very much."

After a short pause, Casey asked, "Will you see her again?"

"I'm sure we'll see each other again, even though we didn't make definite plans. I think you'd like her. She's easy company, attractive, and has a good sense of humor."

"Oh." A short silence filled the air. "Uh, well that's nice."

While stopped at the traffic light, a large truck with a loud muffler pulled up next to Mica. Using the button on the steering wheel of her car, Mica adjusted the phone volume, so she could hear better. "What do you want to do tomorrow?"

"I figured I'd take Grams out for a food shopping expedition and maybe buy her some lunch."

"Want some company? Maybe afterwards we can watch a movie or something back at my place?"

"Super! That would be wonderful. I'll pick you up around ten?"

Mica glanced over at the time on the clock. "That'll work. See you then."

CHAPTER SEVEN

"NEW SHIRT?" CASEY ASKED Mica as she settled into the back seat and buckled up.

"I got it last week. Like it?" Mica reached forward and patted Grams on the shoulder. "Good morning, Grams. How are you feeling today?"

"Not quite feeling myself today. I had a funny spell this morning. I seem okay now, though."

A frown appeared between Casey's eyes. She stopped at the light and looked at her grandmother. "What kind of spell, Grams? You didn't tell me you weren't feeling well."

"I'm not sure. I felt weak all over. I sat down in my rocker, and in a little while, I felt better."

Casey searched her memory for the Stroke Association's acronym, FAST, for symptoms of a stroke. The smile on the wrinkled face seemed symmetrical and her speech seemed okay. "That's good. I think we should take you to the doctor for a checkup though. I'll call when we get settled. Hopefully, we can get in to see the doc tomorrow."

Casey's last comment drew a round of whiney criticism from Grams. "You just had me there last week. Nothing was wrong with me." Grams pulled at her sleeve. "I guess it's not a bad idea though. Today, after the spell, I had a hard time remembering how old I am."

"Well, you're thirty years older than my mom."

"Oh right. She's going to be a hundred eighteen this year. That makes me a hundred forty-eight. No wonder I don't feel as good as I used to."

Casey's almost laughed, until she realized that her grandmother wasn't teasing her. "You look pretty good for that age. I forget...what town is this?"

Confident in her answer, Grams replied, "This is Newark, Delaware. Maybe you should make an appointment for you as well." Grams cleaned her glasses for the third time since she got in the car. "Do you have any aspirin? I have a bit of a headache today."

Grams' response was off by two states. She hadn't lived in Delaware for over forty years. Frequent wiping of her glasses hinted that Grams was having trouble seeing clearly. Then there was the headache and the confusion, as well. "Grams, we're going to make a quick stop before we have lunch." Casey clicked on her blinker and drove as quickly as possible to the hospital.

She pulled into the ER parking lot and took the last fifteen-minute, temporary space available. Mica jumped out and got a wheelchair from in front of the entrance. After her initial protest, Grams acquiesced and allowed Casey to roll her into the hospital, while Mica moved the car to the parking garage.

They went to the reception window where the nurse began requesting information. Grams put her hand to her chest and rubbed. She looked up at Casey. "Honey, would this be a good time to tell you I have a pain in my chest?"

The nurse overheard Grams' comment. Within seconds the staff flew into action. The nurse directed Casey to sit in the waiting room. "I'll be back as soon as we know anything."

Casey found a place with two empty chairs in the corner, anticipating that Mica would be back soon. The shape of the hard, plastic chairs bore no resemblance to the shape of the seated human anatomy, leaving her to shift uncomfortably every few minutes. She glanced at the clock on the wall. The stuck second hand caused a loud tick with the passing of each second.

"Wow!" Casey straightened up from the slump she'd been sitting in, as Mica came rushing in. "That took a long time."

"Tell me about it. I'm parked in a spot so far away, it seemed like it really was in Delaware."

"You *are* the best friend anyone could ever have." Taking Mica's hand into her own, Casey drew it to her thigh and didn't let go. She rewarded Mica's effort with a wan smile.

"Where's Grams?"

"They took her in for some tests. The doctor assured me she'd come back out as soon as she was done."

Mica switched hands and leaned closer, so she could drape an arm over Casey's shoulders. "She'll be fine. I feel it."

It was nearly an hour later that the nurse summoned Casey. "I'll take you in to see the doctor, now." She led them into a small waiting room. A few minutes later, dressed in a white coat that looked two sizes too large, a female version of Doogie Howser took a seat. "Hello, I'm Dr.

Bishop. You can call me Melissa." She glanced down at her notes and got right to the point. "It was wise of you to bring your grandmother in today. She was experiencing atrial fibrillation. That's an irregular heartbeat. Sometimes, the churning of the blood in the heart causes small clots to form. She may have had a TIA or mini-stroke today. Are you familiar with that term?"

"Yes. Will the difficulties she had with confusion and possibly her vision, reverse themselves?"

"She seems to be improving already, which is a good sign. Your grandmother seems clearer now than when she first arrived. We will be keeping her here for observation and some additional testing tomorrow. Depending on the test results, she may be released in a couple of days. You do understand that it is possible for someone who has had a TIA to experience a larger stroke at some future time."

"Yes, I understand."

"We'll be putting her on a blood thinner, and possibly some other medication, to prevent another incident." The doctor reviewed the results of the tests they'd conducted so far, and then offered to have a volunteer take the women up to Grams' room.

They scurried along the hallway, steps behind the young woman. "Here she is." The volunteer pointed to the sign. "Bernice Williams. She's in bed B, next to the window."

After thanking the volunteer who turned to hurry off to her next duty, Casey led the way into her grandmother's room, with Mica following a step behind.

Mica's greeting was relaxed and cheerful. "Hey Grams, how ya feeling?" They approached the bed, and each bestowed a kiss to the parchment-like cheek of the patient.

"I don't understand why I have to stay here. I feel fine."

"Personally, I'm pleased you're here." Casey sat on the edge of the bed, and Mica took the chair in the corner. "I want them to give you a fifty-thousand-mile tune-up and check under the hood."

"Very cute." The feisty old woman waved off the comment with a flick of her hand. "What are they really doing to me?"

Casey met the bright eyes of her grandmother. "They're running a few tests. They think you had a TIA or small stroke."

"I know."

"That you had a stroke? How do you know that?"

Grams raised one shoulder. "I was there."

"Yes, I guess you were." Not sure if her grandmother was being serious, Casey tried not to chuckle and changed the topic. "I hope they're treating you well."

"Do you know they have a man here taking care of me?"

"Yes, I've seen several male nurses on the floor."

"I don't like it. Some guy walked in while I was in the bathroom. He said he was there to help me. I made him skedaddle. I haven't ever dropped my pants for any man I wasn't married to, and I don't intend to start now."

A cough sounded like an attempt to cover a burst of laughter. Casey glanced over at Mica, who turned her head to look out the window in a pointed effort to avoid eye contact. They visited for a couple of hours before Grams' eyes started to droop. They kissed her goodbye and left the hospital.

They were out of breath by the time they made it back to where Mica had parked the car. Casey stopped at the gate to pay the parking fee, and then eased into traffic. "I think she seems pretty normal to me. What do you think?"

"She doesn't seem too much the worse for wear. Earlier, there was something off. Now, for the most part, she seemed normal to me. Unfortunately, the doctor said that this incident could be the precursor to a more serious stroke."

"I know." Casey fell silent, deep in thought. Mica didn't break the silence; she gave Casey the space to work through her feelings on her own. Nearly ten minutes later, Casey reached over and squeezed Mica's hand. "Thank you for being there with me and for all the support you give me. I couldn't have a better friend or partner. I love you."

"Yes, me too, you." Mica flattened Casey's hand on her thigh and covered it with her own. "I know I can depend on you, as well." Mica sighed and changed the subject. "Where are you taking us? How about some lunch?"

CHAPTER EIGHT

THE WEEK FOLLOWING GRAM'S medical incident was an active one. The TIA had left her with a slight balance issue. The doctors decided to put Grams in a rehab facility, so they could more closely monitor her for a month or so. Other than that, she seemed to have bounced back to normal. It took some convincing to get Grams to agree to her 'incarceration.'

Casey met with the therapists at the facility to form a therapy plan for her grandmother. With Grams in rehab, Casey called a friend, a painter by trade, who agreed to do some freshening of Grams' living area.

Mica finished up with her last Thursday morning client and joined Casey in their small break room. She squeezed Casey's shoulder on her way to the mini-fridge. "Want to go out for dinner Friday night? We can catch up on the guest list for our bowling get-together."

Casey looked up. There were dark circles under her eyes. "That would be nice. Do you want to go back to that Italian restaurant where you met your date, Lisa? You said they had amazing food."

"Umm. Yes. The dessert was phenomenal." Mica unwrapped her sandwich. "I'll call for reservations for tomorrow night. Six thirty?"

"Wonderful. I'll pick you up at home around six." Casey folded up her trash.

Almost as a second thought, Mica asked. "Would you mind if I asked Lisa to join us? I think you'd like her, and she says she misses eating out."

"Oh." Casey's jaw muscles tightened. "Of course. Ask her. I don't mind eating at home if you'd rather see her alone." Her eyes searched Mica's face.

"No. I want to go out with you. I just thought, the more the merrier. I'm sure you'll like her. She's very sweet, and I think, a bit lonely. I won't ask her if you don't want me to."

"I'm sorry. It was just a surprise that you wanted to include someone else. It's been only you and me for so long. It surprised me, that's all. Please, invite Lisa, I'd like to meet her." Casey stood up, placed the remnants of her lunch in her brown bag, and tossed it into the trash can. "I'd better get out there." She touched Mica's shoulder as she passed. "I have a client coming in about five minutes. Catch you later. I'll drive on Friday."

***

Theresa Romano greeted the women warmly and showed them to their table. "It's so nice to see you have returned so soon," she said to Mica. "Ms. Taft is already seated. She requested the same server, so I have you seated in Serena's section. Please, follow me."

They were led to a small room in the back of the restaurant, where Serena was chatting with Lisa. Both women smiled as the others entered the area. Serena greeted the women, before she excused herself to attend to her duties.

There were only two other tables in the little alcove. The crisp, white tablecloths stood out against the deep-green walls and created a welcome nearly as warm as Lisa's genuine smile that appeared the moment she saw Mica. "Nice to see you again."

Mica approached and gave Lisa a quick embrace. "Lisa, this is Casey Harrison. Casey, Lisa Taft." The two women exchanged the standard pleasantries, and everyone took their seats.

Lisa reached across the table and squeezed Mica's hand. "I can't tell you how pleased I was that you and Casey asked me to join you tonight." Casey's gaze dropped to the joined hands, then darted to Mica's face. Apparently oblivious to Casey's scrutiny, Lisa was grinning at Mica.

"I'm glad you were available on such short notice. Fair warning, brace yourself. I'm going to order the carbonara this time. Your nutritional reign of terror is over."

Lisa withdrew her hand from Mica's and covered her mouth in feigned shock and horror.

"Don't try to browbeat me. I've already made up my mind." Mica held out her hands, palms up as if balancing something. "I weighed trying to impress you against my craving for my pasta of choice. I'm sorry to break this news...you lost."

Lisa's quick laugh drew a smile from Mica.

"Obviously, Mica, you have internalized my advice from our last meeting and are either walking home or have copious amounts of

38

exercise planned for tomorrow."

Mica's face fell. "Hmm...I'd forgotten that part." Mica glanced over at Casey before she blurted out, "Actually, I do. Tomorrow a group of us are getting together to go bowling over at Murphy's Bowl-A-Rama, at seven. If you like to bowl, you should come."

Mica's eyes darted to meet Casey's, and Lisa's naturally followed. With all eyes on her, Casey swallowed hard. It was a few beats too slow for her response to be considered enthusiastic agreement, but she gamely said, "Yes, definitely. You should come." Casey licked her lips and displayed a more genuine smile. "There are a group of us going. We're trying to fix up my Match Me date with our receptionist from work." She opened her menu. "I know you've already decided what you want, Mica. I think I need to study the menu before Serena returns." Casey disappeared behind her raised menu.

"Casey's date was nice, albeit a bit young," Mica set her closed menu on the edge of the table.

"They seem to make a habit of that. I met my second Match Me date on Tuesday, for coffee. Unfortunately, she was nearly half my age. Thank God that I told the Match Me representative I wasn't available for dinner and only agreed to meet for coffee. My date and I ran out of conversation before the voluminous amounts of sugar she added to her coffee had time to melt. Don't get me wrong, she was very sweet. By the way, her theory about Match Me is that she's the only lesbian in her twenties who applied. Either that, or age was not a high priority in their pairing algorithm."

Casey closed her menu and placed it on the table. "Yes, my date was very sweet too, although not a good match for me. I'm thankful they were offering a special price, so none of us wasted a ton of money."

Serena returned to take their order. Casey and Mica each ripped off a thick slice of crisp Italian bread and dipped it in the seasoned olive oil. Even Lisa managed to enjoy half a piece of bread. As dinner progressed, Casey found herself liking Lisa, despite her initial misgivings. She chastised herself for being selfish and for resenting Lisa's presence in her friend's life. *I love Mica and should want her to be happy and fulfilled. Since we've been spending so much time together, I've grown to rely on her constant and dependable presence in my life.* Casey knew for sure that Mica would always be her friend and business partner. She sighed. *Whatever would I do without the extra special relationship we've shared since we both became single?*

During dinner, they discussed current events and found they all agreed they were happy to see so many women becoming involved in politics since the last election. Several times, Lisa directed questions at Casey in an apparent attempt to pull her more deeply into the conversation. She finally struck on a topic they all enjoyed, their pets. Lisa, too, loved cats.

"I have two rescue cats named Spike and Brutus. They're brothers, although they differ so much in personality that I find it hard to believe. Brutus is the sweetest boy in the world. Spike is constantly in trouble. He loves to watch the wash spin in the machine. Putting the clothes into the dryer always involves a nose count, to be sure he's not jumped in there while I've bent down to get the clothes out of the washer. I can no longer have plants, because he digs them out by the root and does his business in the flower pot. Then there are the blinds. He has one, a particular focus of his mischief, that will never again close properly. He uses it to climb to the top valance, so he can sit up there and survey his kingdom."

Casey warmed to the conversation. "I found Simon at my chiropractor's office during an ice storm. Poor baby was about four months old. He'd been on his own for a while, although he was once someone's pet. He wore a too-tight flea collar when I found him but no ID tags, and he had ear mites. All the patients held him and passed him from person to person as their turn came up. He eventually fell asleep on a boy's lap. The boy wanted him so badly. Unfortunately, his mother said no. In the end, there was nobody who could take him, so I took him in. He's been such a sweetheart. He was so cold and tired that when I got him home, he slept for about twenty hours. Funny, for a cat who obviously once lived outdoors, he's never showed any interest in going out since I brought him home."

Upon Serena's return to remove their dinnerware, they ordered coffee, tea, and a tiramisu. Mica ignored Lisa's raised eyebrow, as she ordered a second dessert for them to share.

The topic changed again to the group bowling event planned for the next evening. "So, Lisa, you never told us if you like to bowl and if you would like to join us." Mica nudged Casey's knee under the table.

Taking the hint, Casey nodded. "Yes, Lisa, join us. It should be fun. Are you a bowler?"

"You're looking at a woman who actually owns her own bowling ball and shoes."

In unison, Casey and Mica gasped, "No!" Making no notice of what they were doing, they linked pinkies.

Lisa chuckled. "I do. However, if I can even find them in my basement or attic, I would almost bet my life savings that the leather has degenerated into something akin to pressed cardboard." A slight smile curved her lips as she remembered happier times. "Suzie and I used to be on the college bowling team. After all these years, the ball I bought then is likely so friable it will shatter like cheap crystal the second it strikes a pin."

Casey perked up. "Who's Suzie?"

"Oh, I forgot you didn't know. Suzie was my partner of many years." Lisa blinked back the tears that threatened and swallowed the lump that suddenly appeared in her throat. "I lost her to cancer." She turned away to remove her wallet from her purse. "I'm sorry to end the evening on such a sad note."

"No, I'm sorry for your loss." Guilt washed over Casey for the slightly cool treatment she'd given the woman earlier that evening. "Let's consider it a pause to our conversation. We can continue our get-together tomorrow, when I suspect we'll all be laughing. I'm lucky if the ball heads down the alley in the proper direction when I release it." They bid good night to Ms. Romano and Serena before leaving the restaurant.

Casey buttoned up against the chill. "I wasn't looking forward to this evening, but you made it fun. I had a nice time."

"Yes, thank you. I enjoyed myself, too. I'm parked right here in front. I was lucky to get the last spot." Lisa turned the collar of her jacket up. "Where are you?"

"We're over there in the lot. I'll get the car." Casey gave a quick hug to Lisa and winked at Mica.

Mica's brows knit together, as she watched Casey's retreating figure. As soon as Casey was out of ear shot, Mica mumbled under her breath, "What the hell was that all about?" She turned as Lisa placed her hand on Mica's arm.

"She thinks she's giving us time alone. She loves you and wants to see you happy. It was very generous of her, considering she's been fighting her jealousy all night."

"Jealousy?"

"Good Lord! You really are oblivious." Under her breath Lisa muttered, "There are none so blind…"

"What?"

"Jeremiah 5:21. Look it up." Facing toward the parking lot, they saw Casey's car approach. "Come here. And don't get the wrong idea about this." Lisa pulled Mica down and placed a quick kiss on her lips. "Unless I miss my guess, that'll get her to thinking." She palmed Mica's puzzled face before giving her a gentle smack. "Now, go be your charming self and get your girl."

"But..."

"No buts. GO!" Lisa gave Mica a gentle push toward the car. She smiled in the direction of Casey's sullen face behind the car window and gave the two women a jaunty wave. Her car horn sounded two short beeps when she pushed the button on the key fob to unlock her own car. She was still smiling as she clicked her seat belt into place.

CHAPTER NINE

CASEY AND MICA WATCHED until Lisa was safely in her car before pulling away. Conversation was nil, with Casey sulking just a little and Mica apparently deep in thought.

Mica finally spoke as they pulled up in front of her apartment. "Thanks for letting Lisa come tonight, Casey."

"I'm glad you invited her and that I got the opportunity to meet her. She's really nice, Mica."

"Yes, I think so, too. I've no doubt she's a kind person with a generous heart."

"Mmm." Casey nodded and reached for the button to unlock the car doors, so Mica could get out.

"What are we doing tomorrow afternoon, after work?"

"I have to go check on Grams."

"Do you want company?"

Casey turned her head away and looked out her side window. She took a deep breath. "Aren't you seeing Lisa? I thought maybe you had a date with her."

"I am seeing her. You and I are both seeing her tomorrow night at bowling."

"Oh, right." Casey's audible exhale seemed to clear the air. "I would appreciate it if you'd come with me tomorrow. I have a meeting with the PT staff, and I'd welcome your opinion on Grams' progress."

Mica reached over and squeezed Casey's hand. "Call me when you're ready to come pick me up."

Casey leaned her head against the cool window glass, as her friend walked up to her apartment door and waved. She could feel her stomach knot with the flood of memories. Seeing Lisa kiss Mica had made her heart ache. Exhaling a long breath, she shifted into drive.

For the first time in years, she thought about Jennifer. What were the chances that she would find herself in the same sticky situation a second time? Was this really the same thing? No. That was a long time ago, when she wasn't even sure she was a lesbian. Jennifer completely discounted the possibility that she could be a lesbian, after all, she 'only really liked dick.' *How many times I wanted to remind Jennifer of that statement. The urge was most pressing every time I buried my head between her thighs. The screams of ecstasy she tried to smother with her pillow indicated that statement was not entirely true.* Casey shook her head. *How young and foolish we were.*

Their friendship began with a shared major and common classes. They sweated and struggled together to master all the muscles in the human body. Their biggest challenge had been to memorize all the protuberances, notches, ridges, and indentations of the bones that their anatomy, physiology, and kinesiology classes required them to learn. Tracing the muscles of each other's bodies led to their first physical intimacy. Neither could remember how things moved to the next level, but they did agree that they couldn't wait for their next 'study session.'

They even went out on double dates together. The minute they returned to their dorm room, they'd crawl in bed and make love until the wee hours of the morning. Like vampires fleeing the first light of the sun, before the alarm rang for class, they'd return to their individual beds and resume their closeted existence, denying the true meaning of their relationship. *So many denials, so many hidden truths, for what?*

She clenched her teeth as she recalled details about the end of their relationship, on the last day before Christmas break of their senior year. Classes were finished. Suitcases were packed and waiting at the door. Later that day, they'd each head home for the holidays. With finals completed, the two women were enjoying the luxury of not having to worry about studies or the need to get up early for class.

Casey lay stretched along Jennifer's side. Her hand trailed the now familiar path over her lover's breast, down her side, and settled between her thighs. "I love touching you." Casey's fingers began to stroke the still damp area, and her tongue reached out to tease an already erect nipple. She raised her head and coaxed Jennifer's mouth with her tongue. "I love you," she whispered.

Jennifer shot up and pushed Casey to the floor. "Don't say that. You can't. We can't." Using her palms, she swept away the huge crocodile tears that filled and then spilled from her eyes.

Suddenly feeling her nakedness, Casey reached for her robe and slipped her arms into the sleeves. She heard the bathroom door close and lock. A few steps brought her to the door. "Jen. Please. Come out so we can talk about this."

Casey heard movement, as Jen approached the barrier between

them. The last sound Casey recalled before Jen opened the door and broke her heart was Jen blowing her nose. Jennifer stood in the doorway in her fluffy, blue robe and fuzzy slippers. She plucked a tissue from the box she had clutched under her arm and dabbed at her tears. "I'm sorry. We can't do this anymore."

"Why?"

"Because I'm not a lesbian."

"Really? You could have fooled me a couple of minutes ago, when I had my fingers inside you and you were biting on the pillow."

Jennifer shuffled over to the bed and sat down. "I'm sorry. I don't want to have this huge secret anymore. I want to have a relationship that everyone respects and approves of. I want kids. I want someone to take care of me and make me feel safe." For the first time since she'd emerged from the bathroom, she raised her eyes to witness the anguish Casey was feeling.

"I can't believe this." Casey slumped down opposite her roommate, on the edge of her own bed. She swiped at her tears with the sleeve of her robe. "I thought we both felt the same about each other. How could I get this so wrong? I love you and thought you loved me."

"I do love you, Case. I love you as a friend. We need to stop, because I can't be your lover after we graduate. You're willing to settle for this..." Jennifer shrugged, "this half relationship."

"That wasn't what I was feeling.'" Casey's tears again betrayed her. "We said we'd always love each other—"

"As friends. I never promised this...this whatever it is, forever. Can't we agree that after we graduate we'll stop this other thing and go back to being just friends?"

Casey shook her head. "No. I don't think so. The way I feel about you, being 'just friends' would feel like a half relationship to me." She stood up and threw on her clothes. Three angry strides later, she stood with her hand on the door handle. Looking back, she met the eyes of the woman she thought she'd love forever. "How could this have gone so wrong?"

Getting no response, Casey grabbed her packed suitcase from where it was resting against the wall and stormed out. She heard nothing from Jen during the holiday break, and her pride prevented her from trying to contact her roommate.

Three weeks later, Casey unlocked the door to her dorm room and put her suitcase on her bed. Her eyes welled up as she saw that every physical trace of Jen had been removed. Wall decorations, pictures, books, and clothing, all gone. On the stripped bed, there was an envelope bearing Casey's name. She flopped heavily onto the edge of the mattress and opened the card. It smelled faintly of Jen's perfume. Casey closed her eyes and inhaled, before she read the card.

Case, I thought it would be better this way. I know you think I don't love you. I do, though not in the way you need me to. I'm sorry, I just can't. If you ever find it in your heart to forgive me, can we be friends?"

A tear dripped on the card and blurred the ink. "No. No, we can't."

CHAPTER TEN

CASEY'S CAR PULLED TO a stop. Mica jumped in and gave her friend a huge grin. She dangled a bag of donut holes from Casey's favorite bakery and offered up her most endearing smile. "Look what I have, your second most favorite sin. My last client canceled, so I decided to run home and change. I stopped on the way and picked these up."

"Thanks. I'm hungry. Was it my imagination, or was it crazy busy today?" Casey looked over her shoulder to check if it was clear to pull away. "I don't think I saw you for more than five minutes all day."

Mica broke a donut hole in half and stuffed it into Casey's mouth like a momma bird feeding her chicks. "You look tired."

"Umph. Water." Casey washed down the mouthful of donut with a huge swig of water. "Yeah, I didn't sleep well last night."

"You were quiet on the way home last night, too. Everything okay?"

Casey tipped her head and raised a shoulder in a sort of half shrug. "Yeah. I guess. I'm not ready to talk about it yet."

Knowing to not push, Mica turned to look out the window. "Okay, whenever. I'm here and hard to get rid of." She was dying to probe, to get at least a small clue about what was on Casey's mind. Instead, she rattled the bag in her hand, "Want more?"

Casey's mouth dropped open and she took a bite of the proffered treat.

"Hey, watch the fingers." Mica was grinning before she popped the remainder of the donut into her mouth.

The meeting at the hospital brought good news about Grams' progress. The lead PT said, "Bernice's core strength is quite good, and her leg strength and balance are already improving. We suggest that she remain at the facility for another week. She could be discharged next weekend, assuming her progress continues at a steady pace. Especially since the two of you have the training to continue her therapy at home."

Casey and Mica made the trip down the long hallways of various pastel hues. They took the 'green' elevator to the residential section and followed the sound of laughter down the hall to Grams' room. The nurse was coming out of the door as they arrived. "That woman is too much. She keeps us all laughing around here." She was still chuckling, as she hurried off down the hall toward the nurses' station.

Grams grumbled a bit about having to stay in the rehab center for another week. She only settled down after Casey explained that she and Mica were the reason her release was only one week away. "We'll continue therapy with you at our Fit As A Fiddle, and I'll stay with you at your house until you're back to full strength."

Turning her head, she peered at Mica. "You staying too? We'd all have fun as roommates."

Before Mica could reply, Casey answered for her. "Mica might be too busy to hang out with us too much." Mica shot a quizzical expression in Casey's direction.

"What did you have for breakfast, Grams?" Casey asked.

Mica didn't know what to think of the abrupt change in topic. A bit more than an hour later, the aide set Grams' lunch tray on her table and lifted the plastic cover. Grams thanked the blue-clad woman and smiled as she left. She curled her lip as she perused the tray. "MREs are probably more palatable than this stuff. I can't wait to get back to my own cooking."

The aide came to collect Grams half an hour after they'd cleared the lunch tray. Casey and Mica followed them to rehab and kissed Grams goodbye. They watched through the observation window, as the therapist put her through various exercises, commenting to each other about how well she was doing. Seeing her friend's concerned expression, Mica draped an arm over Casey's shoulder and felt her stiffen at the touch. *What the hell is that all about?*

"Come on, I'll drop you home, so you can get ready for your date later." Casey ducked out from under Mica's arm and headed for the door leading to the parking lot.

My date? Oh, good Lord, maybe Lisa's right. Casey is jealous. Unsure of how to handle this new wrinkle in their friendship, Mica cautiously blathered on about some nonsensical story she'd recently read in the latest gossip rag. Despite her best effort to extract a laugh from her friend, the most she was able to get was a begrudging smile. As they pulled up to Mica's place, she patted Casey's arm. "Thanks. I'll see you later. I'm looking forward to beating your butt."

For a moment, Casey's eyes sparked to life at the challenge. "You should live so long."

Just as quickly as it came, the light in Casey's eyes extinguished. Mica fought to shake off the sadness that fell over her like a cloak. "You want me to pick you up tonight?"

"Maybe we should drive separately. You might want to stay and hang out with Lisa. I'll see you there later."

Mica swallowed her retort. She stood on the curb, watching Casey accelerate into the distance. Mica sighed and pivoted toward her entryway. Needing to think, she changed into her running gear and started out at a gentle pace, bound for her favorite coffee shop. She slowed to a walk as it came into view and was pleased to find no one in line ahead of her.

"Hi, Mica. What'll ya have?"

"Hi, Sally. Since you don't serve alcohol, I'll settle for a large coffee."

"Oh my. That bad?"

"Not sure, though it's sweet of you to ask." Mica carried her cup to the condiment bar, where she added sugar and grabbed a couple of napkins. She took a seat in the corner and allowed her mind to wander, as she stirred her coffee with the hated wooden stick that carried the danger of impaling her tongue with a splinter. She'd always felt that its inventor should be punished.

Sally approached to swipe a wet rag over the now empty tables and stopped next to Mica. "You look like you've lost your best friend."

Mica smiled. "I certainly hope not." She sighed, snapped the wooden stick in half, and wrapped it in her napkin. Sally responded with a wave as Mica bid her a good day and tossed the half full cup into the bin. As she jogged home, her mind still churned, trying to deal with Casey's distance. She hoped that whatever this was, it would soon pass and not carry over into the office on Monday. She also wondered what Casey was doing.

AJ Adaire

CHAPTER ELEVEN

THE FAMILIAR SOUNDS OF the bowling alley assaulted Casey's ears. She was torn between listening in on Mica and Lisa's conversation and keeping track of how Trish and Nell's discussion was going. Trish was making a heroic effort not to yawn at Nell, who droned on about some 'wonnnderful' band she'd discovered. "TBH, they're the best I've ever heard. I just know when their new song drops, it'll break the internet."

Trish lasered a death stare at Casey, who suddenly found her shoe laces needed adjusting. When she dared to look up, she found Trish scanning the room. *She's probably looking for an escape route.*

Nell stopped her fangirling long enough to check her text messages. "Oh hey, everyone, I'm so sorry. My friend had a flat and I've gotta bounce. I'm so sorry." She grabbed her coat, gave a quick wave, and fled for the exit to a chorus of "bye," "see you," and "drive safe."

Fingers like fierce pincers gripped Casey's upper arm. Trish rasped out an angry threat that included something about Casey paying a debt with her firstborn.

"I told you, if you get past the initial onslaught, she's really sweet. It's not like I held a gun to your head."

"I'm sure she is, but I don't think I'll live that long." Trish shrugged into her coat. "I'm going to pass on bowling tonight. Maybe I can catch up with my friends who went out for a drink or fifteen. I'm already way behind them." She winked and hugged everyone in turn. She whispered in Casey's ear, "I may forgive you someday. Until then, don't eat anything opened or unsealed out of the fridge at work."

The look of shock on Casey's face was apparently the reward Trish sought. Her laughter rang out, making the others wonder what she'd said. Trish's attention drifted to a woman standing near the bar. "Who's that waving at you?"

Four women turned in unison. Lisa was the first to recognize Serena. She smiled and returned the wave. "Hey, let's go say hello."

Serena introduced her friends, Marisol, Sofia, and Beth. By the time the league games ended, and lanes were freed for open bowling, the

51

group members were chatting like old friends. They got two lanes next to each other and team competitions quickly developed. Between turns, Serena and Lisa sat together talking and laughing.

Casey and Mica sat side by side at the table, checking the final scores. Mica announced the totals. "That's one win for each team. Tie breaker?"

Marisol looked at her friends and shook her head. "Sorry, we can't. Early morning tomorrow."

"I'd love to stay if I can catch a ride home" Serena looked directly at Lisa. "Can you drop me? I'm only a few blocks from here. It's probably on your way home."

Lisa glanced over at Mica, whose quick wink and subtle smile seemed to inspire her response. "I'd be happy to drop you, Serena. Let's play another game. I think we can show these youngsters how it's done."

Casey wrote the names on the score sheet. Mica drained the last of her beer and stood up. "I'll go get us another round. Do you both want the same thing?"

"Let's get a snack too." Lisa approached Mica. "I'll come with you to help carry it all."

Lisa and Mica made their way over to the bar and placed their order. The bartender relayed to the cook what they wanted, and while it was being prepared, they had a few minutes to talk. "Someone obviously has an interest in you." Mica smiled and watched as pink crept up Lisa's face.

"We have a lot in common. Because she lost her partner too, we're in the same place in our lives. For her, it was sudden and unexpected. We're not sure which of us had it harder. We just know that living without them is a challenge. She's quite a few years younger than I am. I'm afraid of the age difference. As time passes, we'll see." Lisa shrugged. "Like I told you, I'm only interested in friendship right now." She looked across toward the lane where Casey and Serena sat actively engaged in conversation. "Is Casey still being difficult?"

Mica shrugged. "Things are a little strained, and I'm worried. I don't understand her. Things have suddenly shifted between us, and I'm not sure why. We have no romantic claims on each other, and despite my telling her that you and I are only friends, she still seems jealous of you."

"Maybe over the past months, your friendship moved to a different level in your hearts and your brains haven't caught up to the changes?"

"Hmm."

"Hmm, yes, or hmm no?"

Mica laughed. "I think it's a hmm, I'll have to think about it."

The bartender returned with their drinks. "Order will be ready in a couple of minutes, ladies."

"Mica. If you want to get your friendship back on an even keel, you and she need to have a heart-to-heart and put your cards on the table."

"I'm so worried about how she's reacting." Mica looked across the way to Casey, who was still talking to Serena. "I feel like she's pulling away, and it's not just our friendship that's being affected. We own a business and work together every day. What's that old proverb—don't mix business with pleasure? Someone, long ago, was very wise."

"Although you describe your situation with Casey as a friendship, it's become more than that. I'd say that what you two have is a relationship that's remained nonsexual. You've admitted that you love her, and she obviously has feelings for you. Let me ask you a question. Do you want to continue like that?"

"I don't want to continue like this, for sure."

"You could confront the situation head on. Ask her for a date and tell her how you feel. Then kiss her goodnight and you'll both know if there's more there than friendship."

"I don't know…"

"Food's up." The bartender brought their food order, and they carried it back to the others.

Serena and Lisa won the final game, and the night ended with hugs for everyone. Casey and Mica watched Serena and Lisa's retreating figures walk toward Lisa's car.

"We've met some really nice people. I like them all." Mica bundled her coat closer around her body in the chill night air.

"I don't get you. Aren't you the least bit jealous your girlfriend went off with another woman?"

"Girlfriend? I told you she's a friend. That's all. I mean that."

Casey shrugged against the chill. "I'm freezing. I'd better get going. See you at work." She hesitated for a second, as if debating what to do.

"Come here and give me a hug, you big goof." Mica wrapped her arms around her friend. She buried her nose in Casey's neck and inhaled the familiar, delicious scent. The advice Lisa gave her flooded through her brain. *What would happen if I just kissed her?*

Casey pulled away and broke the moment. "I'll see you. Drive safely."

CHAPTER TWELVE

CASEY LOOKED UP TO greet Mica as she brought her coffee to the table. She even smiled. Days passed, and the week progressed. Each day, Casey's smile seemed warmer and more genuine than the one from the previous day.

Their conversations slowly eased back to normal as well. Well, normal if you didn't consider that Mica couldn't get rid of one particular thought—Lisa's suggestion about kissing Casey. Mica couldn't help herself from staring, as Casey brought her tea to her mouth. As the cup drew closer, Casey's mouth opened slightly, almost as if she were preparing for a kiss. Mica licked her lips.

"What?" Casey stopped, the cup suspended in midair. "Why are you staring at me? Do I have crumbs on my chin or something?"

"No, no crumbs. You…" Mica shook herself back to the real world before she had to wipe drool from her face.

"I what? Spit it out."

"Nothing. I forgot what I wanted to say."

"What's wrong with you?"

Mica reached for her coffee. "Nothing. Everything's great." She pulled out her chair and sat down.

"Grams gets sprung from rehab tomorrow. Can you come and help me get her settled at home?"

"I wouldn't miss it. Were you able to arrange for an aide?"

"Yes. I have one scheduled to start this week. She'll stay with Grams during the daytime. The agency will do a home visit to assess how much help she needs. I think I might stay with her at night, until I see how she does. She seems back to normal, or as normal as she used to be."

They both chuckled. "Oooh. Let's do a cooking marathon on Sunday. If you make Grams' 'roastabeef,' I'll make a vat of sauce. We can freeze it to have for meals later. We can do pork chops and maybe a bunch of meatloaf muffins. She loves those."

"Thanks, Mica. That'll be great." Casey was whistling as she left to care for her patient.

***

Casey and Mica both canceled their last client appointments on Saturday afternoon, so they could leave work early. They drove to the rehab center where Mica left Casey to deal with the paperwork and went to spring Grams from captivity. "Are you ready to go, Grams?"

"I'm happier than a dog with two tails."

Mica was grinning the whole time she tucked the blanket around Grams.

"The way you're wrapping me up, it must be colder than a witch's tit out there."

"Where do you come up with these sayings?" Mica squatted in front of the wheelchair and tucked the blanket around Gram's feet.

Keen blue eyes peered back from the wrinkled face. Deep dimples appeared in her rosy cheeks. "I'm from Delaware, dear. Don't ya know I'm a Belle of the South?"

"Yes ma'am, I do." Mica chuckled.

Casey appeared and wheeled Grams toward the exit, while Mica went for the car. Grams was mumbling under her breath, complaining about not being able to walk to meet Mica. Figuring it wasn't worth the effort, Casey bit her lip and hurried for the door.

Once settled in the car, Grams asked, "Where are we off to? Wherever it is, I hope it involves lunch. I'm hungry enough to eat my socks."

"That's not one I've heard before, Grams." Mica grinned.

Quick as a wink, Grams came back with, "That's 'cause I made that one up."

They all laughed and agreed to Grams' request for Chinese food. They got lunch specials and drove home to her house to eat, because Casey needed to meet with the home health agency. As Casey helped her grandmother out of the car, Grams looked up at the huge, green Victorian house she called home. "I've never been so happy to see anything in my whole life. I feared I'd not be able to return home." She grasped her granddaughter's hand. "Thank you for everything."

Casey wrapped her arms around the humbled little figure as she brushed at her eyes. "Come on, let's get you inside."

Grams held onto Casey's arm as they walked the sidewalk to the house. "I can do it on my own, you know. I just like having you nearby."

Casey and Mica got Grams, all her bags, and the rest of the things she'd accumulated during her stay in the hospital and the rehab facility, through the front door and into the living room. Casey slipped out of her jacket and helped her grandmother into the kitchen, while Mica returned to the car for the food and Casey's suitcase. "Why don't you sit down? I'll get the paper plates, utensils, and napkins."

As Grams settled into her seat, she passed a large burst of gas.

"Grams!" Casey fanned the air with the plates.

"I'm sorry, dear. You'll be old one day too. Blame those people at the home. Who in their right mind would feed baked beans to a bunch of old people?"

***

Casey arranged coverage for the times Grams needed assistance with the home health agency. Grams would spend part of the day receiving therapy at Casey and Mica's place. Before she left, the nurse ordered a medical alert bracelet and explained what it would do for Grams.

"So, I'll be just like Dick Tracy. I can talk into the thing on my wrist."

***

Casey walked Mica to the door and checked her watch. "I can't believe it's only nine. I was ready for bed an hour ago. Tomorrow, I want to get one of those baby monitor things, so she can call me during the night if she needs me. She says she feels capable of being on her own, but I'd rather see her get more of her strength back before we agree to that."

"I'll help out. You know that. I love her, too. I hope I have half that amount of strength of will at her age."

"I know you will. You're always there for me. Don't forget Simon."

"I won't. I'll pick him up from your place on my way home. We'll be good buddies while you're here."

Casey reached her arms around Mica and stepped into her embrace. Her eyes filled as she rested her head on Mica's shoulder and sniffed. Mica embraced Casey, pulling her close, and kissed her on the forehead. For a fleeting instant, she thought of dropping her lips to Casey's. At least she'd know for sure if she was imagining her attraction, or was simply wishing it were so. As she inhaled the scent of Casey's hair, she could feel the beat of her pulse increase.

Casey straightened up and took a step backward. "I'm sorry."

"I'm not. I like holding you. You kind of tuck in at just about the right height. Besides..."

"What? Tell me."

"Not tonight."

"Why?"

"I can't. I will sometime, just not tonight. I'll see you tomorrow around nine...and yes, I'll bring you muffins."

Casey stood watching Mica all the way to the car.

CHAPTER THIRTEEN

"YOU'RE DOING SO MUCH better, Grams. You've been coming to Fit As A Fiddle for a little less than four weeks, and your balance is already back to normal. If you keep working out, you'll be able to challenge Jillian Michaels." Mica helped Grams get off the recumbent cross-trainer and took her by the hand. "It's almost ten o'clock, and the electronic bowling group is getting ready to start."

Grams lifted her head and straightened her spine at the compliment. "You don't have to help me, Mica. I'm sure you have better things to do than lead me around here. I know where to go." Grams, whose stride could be measured with a foot-long ruler rather than a yardstick, hurried over to the corner where the gym assistant was setting up the game.

It was always Mica and Casey's dream to create a gym where older people could keep moving and remain active and healthy. The large room at the back of their PT facility contained treadmills, an electronic-game corner, and a pneumatic, weight training circuit. Across the center of the room, the expense of a whole line of recumbent cross-trainers had proven to be a very popular addition. Mica surveyed the room and gave a nod and a small smile to the clientele, who were socializing as they worked out. Millie, at age ninety-four, was their oldest client. "Look at her, Casey. She and Grams could both be mistaken for someone ten years younger than their chronological ages. I can't get over the fact that Millie drives herself here every day."

"Come on Bernice," Millie called. "We need you on our team. You never miss your pickups."

"That's how I got three husbands," Grams quipped and made the bowlers laugh.

Yes, socializing was a perk at this gym. Plus, there were no serious weight lifters claiming dominance over patrons or the equipment. Their gym, geared to physical fitness rather than body building, had garnered a positive response from within their community and the surrounding areas. As physical therapists, they taught each of their patients how to use the equipment as part of their therapy. When their treatment sessions concluded, each PT client was offered a one-month, free membership at the gym, and most remained members after that.

Casey followed Mica's gaze as her grandmother let out a whoop. "I think she scored a strike. She'll be on the pro circuit soon."

"She won't have time, because she'll be running this place before we know it." Chuckling, Mica looked at her friend who returned her smile.

"I know. Grams is already helping Trish do the filing, and she's damned good at it, too."

"If we're not careful, she'll be providing therapy to the patients." Mica glanced over toward the game in the corner. "Look, she's showing Millie how to get a strike."

"Trish is great with her. I think I need to slip her some extra cash for helping out with her."

Mica put her hand on Casey's arm. "If you've finished with your patients, can we do our meeting?" Every Wednesday and Saturday, the two women met to update each other on their patients' progress, alter treatment plans, or agree to release the patients from therapy.

"Sure. Wow! Saturday already. This week sped by. Give me a few minutes to make notes on my last session, and I'll meet you in the office."

They headed in different directions. Mica arrived first, so she prepared two cups, coffee for herself and tea for her partner. She was setting the drinks on the table, as Casey entered and took her seat. She picked up her cup and blew to cool the hot liquid before she took a sip. "Mmm, perfect. It's been nonstop all morning." She sorted through the mail and tore open the first envelope.

Mica nodded. "Tell me about it. If business keeps up like this, we're going to have to hire another therapist. I'm not complaining about our success, mind you. I don't want to get so big we lose the personal touch. I think that's what helped the business grow."

"I agree." Casey slid half of the mail over to Mica. They sorted through it, separating it into three piles: the ones to be tossed, a pile to be passed on to Trish, and a few for discussion.

"How odd is this? Look what came in the mail today." Casey pushed the letter she'd been studying across the table toward her partner.

"What is it?"

"It's an application from a woman who is seeking a position. Her boss is retiring, and the therapy center where she works has been bought out. She says she's willing to relocate. Her experience and background seem good. What do you think? Read the note attached to the front. She's willing to start part time for a few months."

"Hmm. She has great credentials." Mica flipped through the attached references. "I love this reference she attached from an older gentleman. He's obviously smitten. Want to bring her in and see what she's got to offer?"

"Sure. We've got nothing to lose. We said we wanted to start expanding gradually. Taking on a part-time therapist would be perfect."

They worked their way through the charts, reviewing treatment plans and making notes. They each had a couple of patients they planned to discharge, so they sorted the files between them, each taking her own patients, to begin writing up discharge instructions. Grams was in the discharge pile.

"Thank you for working with her, Mica. You've done a wonderful job. She's probably even in better physical condition now than she was before her TIA."

"It's been my pleasure. She's worked very hard. She stresses to me, daily, how she doesn't want to be a burden on you."

"She'd never..."

"I know that." Mica's eyes softened. "We both love her, Case. Socializing with the other members here and working with Trish on the filing has probably done almost as much as the physical therapy. She seems really happy."

"You know what she did last night? She gave me the boot...told me that although she loves having me there at the house, she no longer needs me at night. She wants me to go home today. She says I look tired and need a rest."

"You have to admit that you've been under a lot of stress lately, working here all day and seeing to Grams' needs all night."

"It's not that I physically have to do anything for her, she's capable of managing her own care, especially with the aide. She enjoys the company though."

"You fix her dinner every night and listen to the stories she loves to tell, even though we've heard them all at least twenty times."

"It's interesting, since she's involved at the gym, there are fewer old stories. Now I hear about the group she hangs with at the gym."

Casey shrugged. "Grams needed me there when she came home from rehab." Running a loving hand over her grandmother's folder, she smiled. "She's no fool, though. She told me that she knows she could have another stroke anytime. In her own words, she wants to be as independent as she can for as long as she can. She said she'll welcome me back when the time comes. Grams is worried she'll lose the group and her job with Trish once her PT ends. I did manage to get her to agree to keeping the morning aide to help her shower and dress, tidy up, and prepare breakfast. After lunch, the aide will drop her over here."

"That's wonderful. Can we afford to pay her something?"

Casey chuckled. "I asked her how much we would owe for her services. She doesn't want money. She wants a title."

"What? Oh no. What'd you tell her?"

"I told her I'd have to talk it over with you."

"Great. Got any ideas?"

"Assistant Data Storage Manager?"

"Oh! How about Customer Experience Enhancement Manager?"

Still smiling over their discussion, they stood up and each grabbed an armload of files.

"Oh, I almost forgot" Mica put her stack back on the table. "I got a text from Lisa a while ago, wanting to know if we could come for dinner tomorrow at her house. Serena is preparing paella from her grandmother's recipe."

"That would be a treat. Hope she's making flan for dessert. Hers is the best. What time?"

Mica checked the text. "They want us there for appetizers by seven."

Since their bowling night, Mica and Casey had gotten together with Serena and Lisa a couple of times when Grams' neighbor was glad to give Casey a night off. Lisa and Serena had come to Grams' house for Thanksgiving dinner, and they'd reciprocated by hosting Christmas at Lisa's. Serena was a fantastic cook and loved entertaining.

"That'll be fun to see them." Casey looked down at the clipboard she carried and checked her schedule. "I have only one more patient today, and then I'll run Grams home. I need to pack everything up and bring all my stuff home."

"Want some help? I can finish up here and meet you at Grams'. Do you need a second car to fit everything?"

"No, thanks. I'm okay. I would prefer you bring my baby home to me instead? I miss him."

"I will. I hate to give him back. Simon's good company."

***

It took several trips for Casey to carry in all the belongings she'd brought home from her grandmother's house. *That's the last of it. I can't wait for Simon to get home.* Casey filled the litter box, poured kibble into the dry food bowl, and put out fresh water. She wanted to snuggle her furry friend. She'd especially missed Simon's early morning visits where he stretched out next to her, put his head on her shoulder, and purred like a V8 engine. Mica's quick knock sounded before the front door swung open.

"We're here," Mica sang from the front hallway. She set Simon's cat carrier on the floor and opened the spring latch on the door. He was very eager to get out and inspect his home for changes.

"Simon! Come see mommy." A streak of black and white ran meowing all the way down the hallway until he reached his owner. He weaved around her legs, meowing, until she patted her chest and called his name. He leaped into her arms and rubbed his face against her chin. He even welcomed all the hugs and kisses Casey bestowed on him and rewarded her with a deep purr.

Mica looked around. "Want me to help you carry these to the bedroom?"

"Oh, please. Can you believe how much stuff I wound up dragging over to Grams' place? All of these things go upstairs." Casey tossed three bags toward the foot of the stairway. She pointed at a cloth sack. "That one goes to the laundry room, and the others go to my bedroom. This one is odds and ends. I'll deal with it later."

Mica picked up the huge, orange laundry bag and started up the stairs to the second floor. Casey grabbed the remaining items and followed behind. "Give me that bag and you take these. I'll start the wash."

They swapped, and Mica headed toward the bedroom, a bag in each hand. She called back over her shoulder, "Should we order a pizza for supper?"

"Nope. Before I left Grams, I took out a container of sauce for her dinner tonight. She was looking forward to making some pasta for herself. I brought home one of the larger containers from the last batch we made. We just need to cook the pasta and we're set."

They had dinner and watched an old movie on demand. "I'd better get going." Mica shrugged into her coat. Approaching the sofa, she bent down to kiss the top of Casey's head and inhaled deeply the scent that was Casey.

CHAPTER FOURTEEN

TWO DAYS LATER, CASEY and Mica were each working with clients, while happy conversations emanated from the group of older folks in the corner, led by Bernice and Millie. Casey checked that her patient had the proper weight set on the shoulder pulley and assigned him three sets of ten reps. "As soon as you finish, Rob, do the usual routine. Get a pack from the chest, ice down, and I'll see you in two days."

"Thanks, Casey."

Casey glanced over at Mica, who was standing near a new client as she worked her knee on the bike, post replacement. The client was making half circles with the pedals. "You're almost there, Tess. Try to make it all the way around." Mica looked toward the door and the expression on her face morphed into something akin to a starving woman spying a delicious morsel within her grasp. Casey watched as Mica closed her gaping mouth and licked her lips. She followed her friend's gaze to the beautiful, dark-haired stranger standing in front of Trish's desk.

The woman gracefully slipped off a long, creamy wool cape to reveal a well-tailored and formfitting navy suit. She wore classy red shoes and...were they really pearls? Casey felt immediately shabby in the sweat pants and collared T-shirts emblazoned with their company logo. Her eyes darted back to Mica, who had tucked in her shirt and was busy smoothing down the front with her hands. It was obviously an unconscious gesture, because her eyes had yet to leave the visitor.

Casey blew out a breath and felt herself relax when Mica's attention was ripped away by her client. *Tess's grip might leave a bruise.* Casey chuckled, as Mica winced and refocused to patiently answer the barrage of questions Tess was firing at her.

If that was their applicant, Eden Royce, there for her interview, she was half an hour early. Casey smiled at her client as she said so long and headed for the reception desk with the clipboard holding Rob's records. Trish could be heard saying, "You can hang your coat there on one of the hangers on the rack." While the visitor walked toward the door and

65

did as directed, Trish's and Casey's eyes followed. Walked was much too mundane a word for the woman's form of locomotion. She didn't sashay, she didn't strut...for those were terms that would be reserved for someone ostentatious and showy. Her walk showed a confidence, a sense of self-assurance, and an underlying abundance of sexy. *Well, why shouldn't she be self-assured? Just look at her. She looks like a dark-haired version of Candace Bergen.*

Trish's voice called Casey's attention away from the rise and fall of the mystery woman's well-toned butt cheeks. "What?"

Trish arched a brow in Casey's direction. She tipped her head toward the woman. "She's early. That's Eden Royce, the noon interview."

"Thanks, Trish." Casey shot her a look of warning, even though she was reasonably confident that Trish would be professional in front of the applicant. "Hello, I'm Casey Harrison. Mica has about twenty minutes left with her client. I'd be happy to show you around, though, if you'd like."

Other than clear lip gloss, the woman wore no makeup over her flawless, creamy complexion. Her navy-blue eyes, that matched her suit, were surrounded by long, black lashes that didn't require mascara. The woman joined her hand with Casey's and parted full, naturally pink lips to reveal white, even teeth. "Hello. I'm Eden Royce. I know I'm a bit early. If you're going to show me around, do you mind if I change into something more casual? I wanted to dress professionally for my interview, despite being more comfortable in my work outfit."

Casey showed Eden to the locker room and went back to wait for her at Trish's desk. Trish wasted no time. "My God, Casey. You can't hire that woman. The men will be too excited to get close to the machines."

"Stop!"

"And look at Mica. I was afraid for a minute there she'd step on her tongue or get it caught in one of the machines."

"We're no better. Listen to us." Casey checked the hallway, and seeing it was still empty, she looked over at Mica. She'd never seen Mica look at anyone like that before. Never, in all the years she'd known her.

Eden presented herself dressed in sweats. Not the average baggy sweats normal people wore to the gym, this was something special. Her outfit screamed custom tailoring and spoke volumes about Eden's pride in her appearance. "Okay." She rubbed her palms together. "Now I feel more like myself." She grinned her disarming smile.

Partly due to Mica's reaction, Casey wanted to dislike the new applicant. However, she quickly warmed to the engaging young woman's wit, knowledge, and ready smile demonstrated throughout the tour of the facility's back rooms. Finished with the behind-the-scenes layout, Casey brought her out into the gym. She guided her through an explanation of how they integrated their patients into the gym area and showed her the private therapy rooms and shower facilities. She loved Eden's easy manner with their clients, several of whom she joked with as they toured through the facility. Eden pointed to Grams' gang in the corner. "I'm dying to meet that group over there. They seem to be having a great time."

"That's my grandmother, Bernice, her friend Millie and their cohorts." Casey led the way over and introduced everyone. Randy lived up to his name as their resident 'dirty old man.' He nearly drooled. Casey watched to see how Eden would deal with Randy. Although he often came on strong, he was harmless. He had a heart of gold and was genuinely well-liked by the group. "How'd you get to be so hot, sweetheart?"

Eden put her hand on the old man's shoulder, neatly keeping him at arm's distance. She looked to the left and to the right, as if she were sharing a secret. "The genie granted me my second wish."

Randy blinked twice and then boomed out a hearty laugh. "Good answer, girlie. What was your third wish?"

"Well, world peace, of course." Everyone joined Randy and Eden in laughter. Eden made her way around the group, and before Casey knew it, they'd challenged Eden to a game. "Do I have time?"

Casey looked at the clock and shook her head. "Sure." Then she admonished the group, "You need to release her in about fifteen minutes, for her interview."

Randy looked up from his job of setting up the game. "Hey, if you don't want her, I'll hire her."

Mica joined her in their office. The large room was painted a restful, pale blue. A sofa separated two desks from the lounge area, and on the other side of the coffee table were two chairs. The room was not used that often, because they preferred meeting in the break room where the table was. Trish pushed open the door, already ajar, and placed on the desk two folders containing their interview questions. "She's on her way."

The interview lasted about forty minutes. Eden's philosophy about therapy and dealing with clients closely matched their own. Her responses were succinct, yet thorough. Her professional experience was broad, although her interests lay in working with older patients. "I indicated that I'd like to start part time. I can do three full days or twenty-four hours a week divided as you need. If you want me an extra day, periodically, I can manage that if you give me notice the week before. I hope that won't be a problem. You see, I'm working on my doctorate with a specialty in geriatrics, which is why I was drawn to your practice. I won't finish until later this year. Right now, I'm working on my project, and I'll stand to defend my research sometime next fall. So, essentially, my hours are flexible and can be based on your needs for now, providing I have time to do my research and write up my findings. My current boss is retiring at the end of the month. The new owner is taking over, so I've been given notice. I can start whenever you need me."

Before the interview ended, they discussed the nuts and bolts of compensation, insurance, and other benefits. They parted with the agreement that Casey and Mica would call her in a few days with their decision once they'd checked her references. They thanked her for coming in and enjoyed the view as she made her way to the door and turned toward the reception area.

Mica ran her fingers through her hair and exhaled a slow breath. "I have to admit my initial reaction was 'wow,' as soon as I saw her. After her interview, I feel the same way. Although now it's because there's a brain behind that gorgeous face."

"Yes, she is bright. And I liked her way with the clients, especially the corner group. She handled Randy perfectly."

"If we'd written up a list of qualifications we need in a therapist, she'd be it. I can't believe our luck. It's a bonus that she only wants part time right now. We can grow her into full time, as we expand and take on more clients over the next few months. You know, kind of ease into adding another employee."

"So, you think we should hire her." Casey fought to balance banning the woman from Mica's sight against the pros of everything that Eden could bring to their business.

"Absolutely. Don't you?"

Casey bit her bottom lip. "I do. Let's divvy up her references and see what they have to say before we make our final decision." Taking the last bite of the protein bar she'd wolfed down instead of lunch, Casey stood. "I've got a client in about thirty seconds. Want to have dinner with me at my house tonight?"

"Uh, sure. Chinese?"

"Great. We can update each other on what we learn from the background checks." As she hurried off to meet her patient, she stopped at the doorway and took in her partner, head bowed over the reference letters. "I'm glad you're coming tonight."

Mica's eyebrows shot up and her head tipped slightly to the side. "Yes. Thanks for inviting me. I guess we've both been busy."

Between patients, Casey made her calls to the two professional references on her list. Both contacts gave glowing reviews. At the end of the day, her final call was to a man named David Bird, whom Eden had listed as a former patient. Unlike the prior two references, the young man revealed he was eighteen. He spoke with admiration approaching awe at how Eden had helped him following a serious sports injury. "I mean, let's be real. Have you seen her? I thought I'd died and gone to heaven." He laughed. "That lasted about half way through the first session. She worked my butt off. I'm sure I was cursing her name by the end."

"And how are you doing now?"

"I'm good as new. I hope you'll hire her, because if anything ever happens to me again, she'd still be close enough to come back to her for therapy. She's the best."

Casey thanked the young man and added her notes to the folder she'd made for reference checks. She gathered her things together and headed for home to tidy up and set the table for her dinner with Mica.

"What's the matter with you? Grams would say you're as nervous as a long-tailed cat in a room full of rocking chairs." Mica deposited the remains of their dinner into the trash and leaned back against the sink. "Are you that nervous about hiring Eden?"

"Possibly, a bit. You know I always worry about finances." Over dinner they'd discussed the results of their reference inquiries and had agreed to hire Eden Royce. They were both concerned about adding another salary to their payroll and agreed they'd wait until Eden got her degree to decide if they'd bring her on full time. "I'll call to offer her the job tomorrow on a part-time basis, with a promise to revisit full-time employment upon her graduation."

Mica looked at her watch. "I'd better get going."

"I'm going to stop and see Grams tomorrow. It's time for another marathon cooking session. Her freezer needs restocking."

"Is that an invitation?"

"It would be fun if you'd come. She loves you, and you always make her laugh. I'll pick you up after lunch. We can shop first and then go to Grams' house."

CHAPTER FIFTEEN

"WE NEED OUR OWN cart boy to help lug all this food into Grams' house." Mica had several bags in each hand, and Casey carried several others. They prepared and cooked her favorite meals...a roast chicken, a pork roast, a huge meatloaf, and a large pot of spaghetti with meat sauce. They carved individual servings, labeled bags, and put them into the nearly empty freezer. Last to finish was the spaghetti sauce. While the sauce cooked down, they took turns stirring the pot and did all of Grams' wash. By the time the clean clothes were folded and put away, the sauce was cool enough to package.

"I've nibbled all day. You girls take home some sauce for your dinner. I don't want to eat tonight." Grams gave them each a hug, and they left for Casey's house. After dinner, Casey threw a load of her own wash into the machine and collapsed on the sofa with Mica.

Mica tipped her head left, then right, stretching her neck. "I think I pulled something lugging all that food into the house."

"Here, turn around. I'll rub it for you." Casey put her back against the arm of the sofa and made room for Mica to slide between her legs. Her touch was gentle, as she worked on Mica's arms and shoulders.

A contented sigh from Mica seemed to indicate that the massage was having a positive effect. "That sounded like a purr." Casey started first at the base of Mica's neck, slid her fingers through Mica's hair, and rubbed her temples before trailing across her forehead. Mica's head fell back onto Casey's chest, as she tucked a hand under each of Casey's thighs and shifted so that the seam of her pants was not putting as much pressure on a particularly sensitive area between her legs.

Casey stroked across Mica's forehead before traveling down to make a brief stop just in front of her ears. Her fingers stroked down Mica's throat to her collar bone, where the previously tight cords in her neck relaxed under the soothing massage. As Casey smoothed the knots from the muscles in the front of her neck, Mica wondered if Casey could feel her heart pounding.

Casey undid the button on Mica's shirt that was impeding her access and slipped her fingers under the neck of Mica's collar to massage where the muscles attached along her collar bone just above her breasts.

A moan escaped from Mica, freezing Casey's fingers. "I'm sorry." She quickly pulled her hands from under Casey's collar. "I...uh...I just wanted to make you feel better. I didn't mean to get so intimate." She pushed Mica's shoulders away, slid her leg out from behind her, and popped up like a cork, briefly covering her flushed face with her hands.

Mica, too, stood up and wrapped her resistant friend in her arms. "Stop. Nothing happened. We're friends. It was my fault. I think I was enjoying that a bit too much." As Casey relaxed and her breathing slowed, Mica loosened her grip. She leaned back and sought Casey's eyes. "We okay?"

Casey nodded and returned to the sofa. "I think you should go. We're both tired and..."

"Sure." Mica walked over to the chair, picked up her jacket, and shrugged into it. Mica could feel Casey watching as she zipped up. Her eyes darted away the minute Mica looked up.

Approaching the sofa, Mica bent down to kiss the top of Casey's head and allowed herself the luxury of inhaling the scent that was Casey.

"Don't forget we're invited to Lisa's tomorrow. Want me to pick you up?"

"No, I'm going to stop in and see Grams first. I'll meet you at Lisa's."

CHAPTER SIXTEEN

CASEY LEFT HERSELF TWO hours for a visit with Grams. She hadn't mentioned the visit, so she and Grams were both surprised when Grams announced that she was expecting company for dinner. "Who's coming?" Casey asked.

"Millie is coming over for a visit. I've got all that food you and your girlfriend made me, and thought I'd fix her a nice home-cooked meal."

"My girlfr...oh, you mean Mica?" Were people seeing things that she was unable or unwilling to see? Or maybe she was hearing something Grams hadn't intimated with her innocent statement.

She stayed a half hour, until Millie was due, before she kissed her grandmother goodbye and got into her car. Feeling at loose ends, she called Lisa and explained she needed to get out of Grams' way. "I know I'm not due for over an hour. However, I'm already half way to your house, and I hate to go all the way home and..."

"Oh, wonderful. Come early. It'll be good to see you. Serena and I are sitting here having a glass of wine."

Lisa lived in a nice section of the city in a too-large-for-one-person, three-story, brick townhouse. One night, over drinks, she'd told Mica and Casey that she just couldn't bear to part with her place and give up the memories. "Suzie and I had mortgage policy and life insurance, so when she died, our mortgage was paid in full. Even though I know it's too big for me alone, it's something I can easily afford. I hope that someday I'll be ready to share it with someone special." When they were alone, Mica had suggested to Casey that Serena might be the perfect person to do that.

Doing as Lisa suggested, Casey pulled into the driveway at Lisa's house. Earlier, Lisa had thoughtfully grabbed a spot on the street while neighbors were out and about running errands, so her guests wouldn't have to search for parking. Serena's car was parked in the open garage, leaving room enough in the driveway for the other cars. Casey rang the bell and handed over the bottle of wine she'd brought. Her hostess greeted her with a warm hug and kiss on the cheek.

"Thank you for the wine. We're in the kitchen. I'm watching Serena cook." Her eyes twinkled, and she dropped her voice to a whisper, "It's a wonderful view. Wait till you see her." She took Casey's coat and over her shoulder she called, "Serena, Casey is here."

While Lisa poured her a glass of wine, Casey took a seat on the sofa. She smiled as Serena came in from the kitchen wearing a white apron with rainbow-colored letters that said, *I kissed a girl...*Serena approached Lisa, slid an arm around her, and gave her a squeeze and a kiss on the cheek.

"Cute." Casey pointed to the words on the apron.

"Not mine." She grinned and looked in Lisa's direction, her eyes soft and expressive. "I do like it though." She laughed. "Both the apron and the kissing a girl thing, especially this one." Serena sat on one of the rockers opposite the sofa, flanking the fireplace. "Everything is ready to cook. I'll start it as soon as Mica gets here."

"Good." Lisa reached for Serena's hand. "You have a few minutes to chat. You've been working too hard."

Settled on the sofa with Serena, Lisa toasted Casey with her wine. "Thank you for coming. It's nice for both of us to have people to socialize with again." Lisa's phone dinged. She picked it up from the table and checked the text. "Mica's on her way. She'll be here in about twenty minutes."

"Oh good." Serena stood and picked up her wine glass. "I hope you'll excuse me. I can't wait to get things started." She trailed her fingers along Lisa's shoulder as she passed.

Lisa's gaze followed Serena until she disappeared out of sight around the corner before she returned her attention to her guest. She found Casey watching her, left eyebrow raised in an unspoken question.

"It's not what you're thinking. I won't deny that we have feelings for each other. I don't want to get involved and then get cold feet. The last thing I want is to hurt her, so we've agreed to give things a little more time. I want to wait until I'm sure I'm ready to move forward. I'll be the first to admit that we're definitely having fun together."

"From the electricity in the air, I can't see the next step being too far in the future."

"Oh, there's no doubt my body is ready to move forward. If only I could get my head, my heart, and my body on the same page." Lisa looked at her watch. "Why isn't Mica with you?"

"We're driving separately. I had to see Grams."

"I'm surprised she wasn't with you to help out. Mica's been quite worried about you lately. She's concerned about how tired you've been."

"I'm okay." Casey stood up and walked to the mantle. "Do you want me to poke at this fire for you?"

"No. I'd rather you come sit down and talk to me."

Casey took her seat and ran both hands through her hair. "I don't know what to do about Mica. Something weird happened between us last night. We've always been affectionate with each other. Last night I..." Casey leaned her head back on the chair and looked at the ceiling. "Her neck was sore, and I was massaging it for her." She held her hands out in front of her. "I, uh..." Casey pressed her palms together and dropped them into her lap before she searched Lisa's face. "I very nearly slid my hands down over her breasts. I don't know what came over me. It's like my fingers had a mind of their own, took over, and betrayed me."

"Have you talked to Mica about what happened and how you're feeling?"

"Recently, no. She knows how I feel. I know Mica told you what happened and how badly my roommate, Jennifer, hurt me. I vowed I'd never get involved with a friend again. In fact, I've barely had any kind of serious relationship since. I've been with my share of women. I just can't seem to allow myself to be vulnerable with them. With Mica, it'd be worse. Not only is our friendship at risk, we own a business together. I'd never want anything to ruin either of those things."

"You know that Mica isn't anything like Jennifer though, don't you? By not being willing to take a risk with Mica, you might be giving up a chance for real happiness."

"I know that, in my heart. We're quite the pair, aren't we, Lisa? We both think too much."

"Isn't it odd that we've become friends? I remember the night we first met." Lisa laughed as she recalled the evening. "There were several times I feared being turned into a pile of salt by the hateful glances you directed my way. There was a distinctly green aura around you. I'm so glad things are different between us now."

"Me too. Thanks for listening."

"Talk to her, Casey. She loves you. In my opinion, you run a bigger risk of hurting each other by not talking about what the two of you are feeling."

The doorbell interrupted their conversation. Mica greeted Lisa with a hug. She looked at Casey and asked about Grams.

"She tossed me out so she could entertain Millie."

Mica laughed. "You'd better watch those two. Thelma and Louise are liable to jump in Millie's car and head for the casinos."

The three women moved to the island separating the kitchen and dining area where they would eat their meal. Serena had set up several appetizers on the counter, and the evening of feasting began.

***

"That was delicious." Lisa smiled at Serena and the other two guests were quick to add their voices to the praise.

"My grandmother taught me this dish. She was a wonderful cook. I miss her very much. She and Bernice would have been great friends with their funny wisecracks. My *abuela* was so subtle with her humor. When Mama gave her a hard time, she would just smile and look her in the eye before she dropped her chin to her chest. Mama always assumed she had the better of her. Then, in a whisper, Abuela would utter a hilarious comment under her breath that would make me have to bite my tongue not to laugh and get us both into trouble." Serena folded her napkin and placed it on the table. "Mama and I used to enjoy cooking with my *abuela*."

Lisa reached over and put her hand over Serena's. "Maybe your parents will come around someday."

"I would like to think that. Attitudes in the Hispanic community are changing all the time, and acceptance for homosexuality has grown so much in the past ten years. Sadly, it hasn't touched my family yet. Until that time, I will be happy with my friends and my family of choice. Speaking of chosen family, have you decided to join us for New Year's Eve?" Serena's hopeful expression brought a smile to Lisa's face. "Don't forget to bring Grams and Millie."

Serena looked to Mica who nodded. "We'll be here. What can we bring?"

Lisa and Casey discussed the logistics for New Year's Eve, while Mica helped Serena clear the dishes. "Casey, you got your wish," Mica called. Serena brought out a thick and creamy flan.

CHAPTER SEVENTEEN

"WHAT TIME ARE YOU coming over here to pick us up for New Year's Eve?" Grams never identified herself on the phone, she just started talking and expected Casey would know who it was. "I have something I want to talk to you about."

"What is it?"

"It's not earth shattering, just something I want to tell you about. Millie will be here soon, and we're going to celebrate, so we'll need you to stop for a bottle of champagne."

"Okay, Grams. I'll try to get there early." *What in the world could those two old ladies be getting up to now?*

"I hope Millie isn't going to drink and then drive home."

"I've asked her to stay over."

"Good idea. I'll see if Mica can be ready early. I still need to stop by and pick her up, and now make an extra stop at the liquor store to replace the bottle of champagne you are drinking. I'll get there as soon as I can."

"Since you're going to go to the liquor store, you might as well pick us up some scratch-off tickets. Can you get me ten bucks worth of that new game—Money For Life, or something like that? It's worth five million."

Casey rushed to get ready. Everything conspired against her, and she was running late as she hurried to Mica's house.

Mica ran out as Casey pulled to the curb. "We have one more stop to make." Casey told Mica about the conversation with Grams as they drove. They caught every red light but finally pulled into the liquor store parking area. "Jesus, are they giving booze away, and nobody told us?" After the third time circling the lot, she gave up and tucked into the end of a row in an illegal space. "Do you mind going? Take my wallet. And don't forget those lottery tickets she wants. Pick up ten dollars worth for me, too. That'll be fun."

As they pulled out into traffic, they saw a pristine, '71 baby blue Mercedes buzz past them. They followed a few car lengths behind.

AJ Adaire

"Millie loves her Pagoda." Mica grinned.

"Yes. You know, she had somebody install a mechanism to raise and lower the top automatically when she got too old to do it herself." Casey looked down at her speedometer and laughed. "She has a bit of a lead foot. She's consistently doing three miles per hour over the limit."

"You have to admit though, she's a decent and courteous driver. She uses her signals and stays to the right except when she's passing."

"Grams told me Millie is a good driver and recently had her license renewed. I admit I feel better having seen her drive for myself. I know Grams misses driving."

"I wonder what we'll do when we're their age?" Mica touched Casey's leg. It was a nonchalant gesture they'd have made without a second thought before the massage incident. Things were still a bit strained between them. *What in the world was I thinking? She looked down at her traitorous fingers. It was as though they had a mind of their own.* As Casey felt herself warm to Mica's touch, she gripped the wheel more firmly and exhaled a sigh of relief when Mica withdrew her hand.

They pulled up behind Millie and watched as she wheeled her suitcase up to the front door. Mica gathered up the champagne, put it on the floor of the passenger's side, and came around the car to meet Casey. "Here's that ticket."

"Ticket? As in one ticket?"

"Yeah. They were ten bucks for one. The prize is five million dollars though. I stuck yours in your purse, along with your change."

Grams was standing at the front door. "You took your good old time. I told you I had something I wanted to talk about. Come into the kitchen. We don't have time to waste. I don't want to be late to Lisa's house and ruin their meal."

Mica and Casey exchanged a look. Mica whispered, "Who stepped on her tail?" Casey stifled her giggle and earned a dirty look from Grams. "Come on."

"Be right there. Let us get our coats off." They followed her into the kitchen and obeyed orders as she pointed to the chairs. "You, sit."

Mica set the champagne on the table and obeyed.

Casey offered the lottery ticket.

"You just got one?"

"You told me ten dollars' worth. There it is."

Grams sighed. "Oh, never mind. I hoped we'd have some time, so I could lead up to this gradually, you know, kind of give you a chance to get used to things. Now we're late and I'm going to have to blurt it out."

78

Grams drew herself up to her full five feet, and Millie came to stand, shoulder to shoulder, next to her. "I've asked Millie to move in here with me."

Casey's mouth dropped open.

"Before you say anything, can I tell you somethin'?" Millie pulled out a kitchen chair and touched Grams on the shoulder. "Come on, now. Sit down and let's tell them why." Casey started to speak, but Millie raised her hand. "You young folks don't know how lonely it is to be old and living on your own. I know this might seem rash to you, because I only met your grandmother a couple of months ago." Millie glanced over at her friend. "I didn't know how unhappy I was until we became buddies. Now we laugh all the time. I used to dread breakfast, lunch, and dinner alone. Now we take turns cookin' dinner. We watch the news and talk about current events. We try to answer the questions on *Jeopardy* and cheer for our favorite contestants on *Wheel*."

Casey looked at her grandmother, then back at Millie. "I do understand what you're saying, Millie. What will you do with your place?"

"My apartment building is goin' co-op. I don't want to own. It wasn't long ago I sold my house because I didn't want the responsibility anymore. Now, I'm back at either having to buy or move."

Casey put her head in her hands and brushed her fingers through her hair. "I don't know…"

"Look, Casey. I'm sure you have all sorts of doubts. You're probably thinkin' these two old women have lost their minds, or you're worried I might be takin' advantage of your grandmother. Let me assure you, I have enough money to support myself. My husband was an investment banker. I'm very comfortable financially and can afford to live where I want. I got an efficiency, because I didn't want to take care of more than that. The news that I had to find another apartment sent me into a tail spin. I dreaded huntin' for another place to live. Bernie suggested I take a couple of rooms upstairs, here in her house."

Casey glanced at the stairs.

Grams followed her gaze. "I'm having a stair glide installed on Friday. There's more than enough room for both of us here to have some private space, if we want to be alone. The important thing is that we enjoy each other and have fun together. We both enjoy jigsaw puzzles and cards." Grams reached for her granddaughter's hand. "I'm not asking for your permission. I do hope for your approval, though."

Casey's eyes filled. "I'm sorry you were lonely. I feel…"

"You've done everything you can, honey. I know that. I think this will be good for Millie and for me." Grams glanced at her friend.

"If it isn't, what have we wasted? Nothing. Your grandmother and I are both adults. I can always find another place if she grows tired of me being underfoot."

"That's not going to happen." Grams stood up. "There's one more thing before we have to go. We're taking a trip, leaving three weeks from now, for fifteen nights on a cruise from San Francisco to Hawaii. We may spend a few days in the wine country before the cruise. I'll give you a copy of our itinerary as soon as we have things firmed up."

Who is this woman and what has she done with my grandmother? Casey stood up and hugged Grams. "I want whatever will make you happy. And if you are both happier doing this, that's a bonus."

"Give me that ticket, Millie. Maybe I'll be able to pay for our cruise." A few scratches later, Grams swore. "Damn. For ten dollars, you'd think I'd at least have won something."

"Don't worry about it, Bernie. We can hit the casino later this week. Maybe we'll have better luck there."

***

The dinner that Lisa and Serena prepared was delicious. Casey and Mica volunteered to do the dishes. "Thanks for offering to help me, Mica. I was hoping we could talk. What do you think about Grams and Millie moving in together?"

"It seems they've got everything worked out between them. They get along well, laugh a lot, and they're right about companionship. Look how much happier Grams has been since she started helping out at the gym."

"It's true. They've got a neat little group of seniors showing up for the games they organize. Initially, I thought we were doing it to keep Grams occupied. Now, I don't know what we'd do without the two of them. I can hear Grams and Trish laughing as they do the filing."

Lisa brought in the last load of plates from the living room. "Mica, when are they announcing the winner of the Match Me contest?"

"They said it'd be on January thirty-first. They wanted the winner known before Valentine's Day."

"We have a while to go yet."

"Lisa!"

"Coming, Millie" Lisa returned to the living room to see what was up. Seconds later, Lisa called to the kitchen. "Can you two bring another bottle of champagne in with you? It seems Millie and Grams are running low."

The women talked and danced and watched the celebrations on TV. Lisa filled everyone's glasses with the final bottle of champagne while the others watched Millie and Grams jitterbug to one of the popular rock songs of the fifties.

Casey had been drinking ginger ale all night. "Just a half for me, please. I'm driving." She noticed the lingering glance Lisa exchanged with Serena, as she topped up her glass.

Mica led the toast as everyone clinked glasses for the New Year's. "Three minutes. Everyone up." They watched as the crowd counted down, and they joined in at ten...nine...eight, until the ball dropped to the bottom and the fireworks started. Lisa and Serena gave each other a quick kiss on the lips. Grams and Millie hugged each other and started around to give each of the women a hug. As the others celebrated, Casey and Mica exchanged their New Year embrace. Mica leaned in and placed a quick kiss on Casey's lips. It seemed like the moment froze in time, as the two women separated millimeter by millimeter. They stared deeply into each other's eyes, until Grams and Millie grabbed each of them by the elbow for their hugs.

CHAPTER EIGHTEEN

MICA HAD ALREADY STACKED the client folders for their meeting when Casey came in.

"Before we begin, I need to ask you a personal question. Are you still coming with me to drop Grams and Millie at the airport, on Tuesday? We'll need to change our afternoon appointments if you're still coming."

"Oh, right." Mica looked up. "They're leaving for their cruise. Sure, I'll come. We both agreed to take them when they announced the trip." Before their kiss on New Year's Eve, there would have been no question of Mica joining Casey to take Grams and Millie to the airport. Although they still saw each other frequently, they were either socializing with Lisa and Serena, or having dinner in a restaurant. They didn't hang out together at home anymore.

"I know. I wanted to be sure. I didn't know if you'd made plans with...uh, Eden or someone else."

Mica rose to walk over and look out the window. "Eden? I helped Eden move into her new apartment and she treated me to dinner as a thank you. She's just a friend, Casey. I suspect that her boyfriend would take exception to me taking her out." She exhaled a long sigh. "I'm not seeing Eden or anyone else, so what plans would I have?"

Casey's eyes opened wide. "No need to take my head off. I'm sorry. I don't know what's happening anymore."

Mica turned around and met Casey's eyes. "No, I'm guilty too. I should be the one apologizing. I'm afraid we're losing us. After the massage, then New Year's Eve...well, we never talked about what happened. It's like we're afraid to be alone. We've been walking on eggshells."

"You're right. I feel like it's all my fault. Let's get together later this weekend and clear the air. I miss us, too."

"I think that's a good idea." Mica exhaled a breath and rubbed her palms together. "Let's deal with Grams and Millie first. Will you have room for me in the car? I'm sure they'll be bringing bags and bags with them."

"You know I hate to drive to the airport. We'll make room if I have to strap myself to the bumper while you drive."

Mica smirked. "I know. Speaking of driving. Do we want to let Lisa and Serena know we might be late? We may hit traffic coming home, and we're due at Lisa's to find out who won that island vacation."

Casey smiled. "I talked to them already. They'll go ahead and eat. They'll have dessert with us while we wait for the winner to be posted."

***

The car tires were nearly flat, and the engine was groaning when they entered the throughway bound for the airport. Casey's trunk was stacked to overflowing with luggage, and two bags that wouldn't fit sat on the back seat between Millie and Grams. "I'll tell you right now, you ladies have overpacked. Grams, you may need to mortgage the house to pay the excess baggage fees."

"I packed my old, ratty underwear." Slightly hard of hearing, Millie raised her voice to assure she was heard in the front seat. "If we need room for souvenirs, I'll toss some overboard."

"I can hear it now. 'Captain, are those whitecaps on the ocean? No, son, I believe those are Granny panties floating on the waves.'" Mica stifled a grin. "I hate to think of you two ladies wandering around that fancy ship in ratty old underwear. What happens if you fall and they take you to the ship's infirmary?" She glanced in the rearview mirror to enjoy the two older women staring at each other with shocked expressions.

"We may have to rethink this plan." Millie took out a pen and tablet with her list of things to remember. "We can buy new drawers while we're in San Francisco."

Mica continued her gentle teasing. "How are the two of you going to manage all these suitcases? Don't go picking up some young stud of sixty to help you. There's stranger danger out there, you know."

"Sixty?" Millie scoffed. "If I pick anybody up, he'll not be a day over fifty and will be well built and strong. If all else fails, that's what bellboys and money are for."

"Ow!" Mica's outright laughter was punished by Casey, who pinched her leg before turning her head away to hide her own grin. It didn't work; Mica saw. The rest of the ride was uneventful. With the luggage checked in, Grams and Millie had boarding passes in hand. Casey and Mica hugged the travelers and bid them a safe trip.

"Their flight is on time. Hopefully they'll have a good time." Casey sniffed back a tear, as they watched the pair pass through security and on to their journey. "I feel like I'm sending my toddler off to school for the first time."

Mica wrapped an arm around Casey's shoulder, forgetting that her gesture might be misinterpreted. "Come on, we need to hustle if we're going to beat the traffic."

They stopped for a quick burger and arrived at Lisa's house a few minutes before seven.

Lisa met them at the door with a beaming smile and warm hugs. "Come on in. Wine?"

"Please," they exclaimed in unison. Each took a seat in the chairs that flanked the fireplace. They talked with Serena, who was sitting with her feet tucked into the sofa. Lisa returned seconds later, with two glasses and an opened bottle of wine. As Lisa poured, Mica and Casey recounted the story of their trip to the airport, including the floating underwear.

Lisa sat close to Serena, leaving the end cushion empty. Wine glass in one hand, she slipped her free hand into Serena's. Their eyes sparkled, as they exchanged a shy smile.

Casey and Mica looked at each other and back to Lisa and Serena.

Serena raised her glass. "Will you join us in a toast? To us."

Casey and Mica raised their glasses and joined in the celebration of their friends' new relationship. "We're so excited for you," Mica said.

"I decided I wasn't getting any younger." Lisa set her glass on the coffee table. "I finally realized that there was room in my heart to still love Suzie and what we had, while at the same time, moving my life forward with Serena." Lisa turned as Serena added to her thoughts.

"We're still taking things slowly. Although, I will tell you what I told Lisa. She'll have a very hard time getting rid of me now."

"I have no intention of trying." Lisa pulled Serena's hand to her lips. "She's right. We aren't getting a U-Haul just yet, even though it is hard to watch her leave some nights."

The rest of the evening went quickly. Lisa got her laptop and set it on the dining room table a few minutes before nine. "They said they'd post the winner of the Match Me vacation at nine, right?"

"That's what the contest rules said," Mica stood up and

approached Lisa. "Let's see if they've announced who won the contest yet." Lisa opened her laptop and passed it to Mica, who quickly navigated to the website. "Oh my God. I can't believe it." Mica stepped back. "Oh man!"

"What? Tell me you won." Casey said, as the others made similar statements. They gathered around to peer at the screen.

"No, none of us. Look at the announcement." Mica reached out her finger and tapped the name listed as the winner. "Cornelia Foster." Mica whispered, shaking her head. She grasped each side of her face. Her disappointment was mixed with mild annoyance at who had won the trip.

The others laughed as Mica groaned. "Can you imagine being on an island vacation with her? Only the two of you for nearly *two endless weeks*? You'd have to wear noise cancelling headphones."

Casey put her hand on Mica's shoulder. "I'm sorry you didn't win, Mica. I know you had your heart set on going to the Keys."

"Oh well." Mica shrugged. "You know I'm a firm believer that if one door closes, another one will soon open."

As they prepared to leave, Mica and Casey hugged their friends, again wishing them happiness and success with their new relationship. Casey held out her hand for the keys to her car and Mica handed them over. At first, the ride home was filled with chatter. "You know what Lisa told me while I was helping her prepare the dessert?" Casey asked.

"What?"

"She told me that they talked about Serena moving in with her. Serena has that efficiency apartment, and Lisa has that huge house. Lisa was reticent to entertain the idea, thinking Serena wouldn't want to live with Suzie's 'ghost.'. Serena has no problem living in a house Lisa shared with someone else. She told her there's only good in the house, because Lisa and Suzie had a wonderful relationship and had made a happy home. Serena feels that same happiness would carry forth for them."

"That's sweet. We do more with them than with any of our other friends. They've become our best friends, and I'm thrilled for them."

"Yes, me too." Casey made the final turn.

Mica looked away, out the side window of the car. Minutes passed. In a soft voice Mica shared her thoughts. "They've been so good for each other. They started with a friendship. It's been fun to watch their relationship grow from a friendship into something more meaningful."

Casey sucked in a breath. The quiet tone Mica used struck harder than if she'd screamed "It's your fault." Although Mica's tone wasn't accusatory, Casey still felt the weight and burden of guilt. She knew she was the one standing in the way of their own relationship. She was the one who didn't trust Mica enough to take the risk.

Her fear had already impacted their friendship. Following her near loss of control the night of the massage, and the electricity of their all-too-brief kiss on New Year's Eve, she could no longer deny the obvious attraction between them. How long could that go unrecognized? To protect themselves from feeling rejection and hurt, surely one of them would back away. Would her jealousy push Mica away? Would it be worse to lose their friendship because they took a chance or because they didn't?

As Casey pulled to a stop, Mica asked, "Do you want to come in?"

Casey checked the clock on the dash. She needed time to think. "It's nearly ten. Let's leave things go for tonight. Tomorrow is our late night at work, and Thursday I have a dental appointment. Can you come for dinner on Friday?"

"Don't be upset...I have plans with a friend for dinner."

"Why should I be upset? Anyway, I need to do some cleaning and cooking before my house is ready for company. I've been so busy getting Grams and Millie settled, there's no doubt my place needs attention. I'd bet you could stuff a full-sized teddy bear with the dust bunnies under my bed. Can you come for dinner Saturday night?"

"Sure. That's fine. See you tomorrow." She sat for a few seconds, her hands in her lap. Instead of reaching for the door handle, she touched Casey's arm. "We're okay, aren't we?"

"You never need to ask." Casey covered Mica's hand with her own. "See you in the morning, at work." She watched until Mica closed her front door before she pulled away. There was a lot for her to think about on her way home. Mica's comments about Lisa and Serena starting their relationship from a friendship felt like a physical blow.

Casey's mind churned the entire way home. Once inside, she put on the water to boil for tea and forced her racing mind to slow down and start at the beginning. Her eyes teared as she allowed herself to recall the day Jennifer broke her heart. She dropped her head into her hands. "Oh my God!" It finally struck her that the painful ending of that relationship had been the reason she'd rarely allowed herself to have romantic feelings for anyone since then.

Self-doubt, and the jealousy it caused, had ruined every budding relationship she'd ever attempted. The closest and deepest relationship she'd ever had was with Mica. If she wasn't careful, her inaction and jealousy might ruin what they shared even before they had a chance to explore if there was more between them than friendship. *I've been such an idiot.* A sudden idea shot into her head that needed some time to execute.

CHAPTER NINETEEN

ON SATURDAY, AT WORK, Mica and Casey sat together having lunch. They could hear Grams' group through the open door. They were only slightly quieter without Grams and Millie. Casey took a drink from her water bottle. "They're doing great, aren't they? The socialization here is wonderful for all of them. We've struck on a good thing for the seniors. Grams met Millie through that group. She told me she's so relieved to not be alone anymore, especially overnight."

Mica chuckled. "That Millie is a live wire. I think the friendship has been good for both of them. Did you know that she and Grams plan to start inviting some of these people over to the house for games on Sunday afternoons? I guess they have some Uber guy who is willing to pick up the ones who can't drive."

Casey popped a grape in her mouth. "Umm hmm. They even arranged for Randy to run the games here at the gym while they're away on their cruise."

"Eden helps keep him in line. He follows her like a puppy. She really has him wrapped."

"Eden has been a gift from some God that has taken favor on us." Casey chewed another grape. "She fits in like she was born here."

Instead of continuing the conversation, Mica returned to reading her paper.

Casey studied her friend. *I'm ruining everything with my stupid relationship rule.* "Mica, you're still coming tonight, right?"

"Yup. I'm looking forward to seeing Simon. I miss him."

Casey felt a sudden pain in her heart. Knowing Mica hadn't meant the statement to be hurtful didn't make the sting any less painful. She wanted to hear that Mica had missed her too.

***

Instead of heading home after they'd closed the center, Casey zipped downtown to a coffee shop to meet Nell. The meeting was brief.

The minute she could break away, Casey was out the door.

Casey hummed a happy tune as she thought about the surprise she would soon share with Mica who was so disappointed when the winner of the vacation from Match Me was announced. Casey reached out to the winner, Nell. A brief conversation with the young woman revealed she had yet to meet anyone to go with her and was thrilled at Casey's offer to buy the trip from her. At least that was what she interpreted Nell's comment "OMG, that's epic" to mean.

Before Mica was due to arrive, there remained only an hour for her to finish tidying, throw the dinner into the oven, and set the table. The stack of unread newspapers on her coffee table revealed how busy Casey had been the past couple of weeks, helping Grams get ready for her new roommate. She lifted a pillow to fluff it and the purse she'd not used since New Year's Eve, fell to the floor.

Casey swore under her breath, as the contents spilled out onto the rug. She stooped to collect the lottery ticket and change Mica had tucked inside at the liquor store before Lisa's party. Casey threw the change back into the purse, tucked it under her arm, and grabbed the stack of newspapers to put in her recycling bin. In the kitchen, she checked the clock and realized there was barely time to have a shower before Mica arrived. The lottery ticket got tossed on the table to be dealt with when she had more time. With the purse in her hand, she rushed up the stairs to take her shower.

• • •

Mica arrived fifteen minutes early and spent the extra time petting and playing with Simon. Dinner conversation included generalities like the weather, clients, Grams, Millie, even Eden.

Casey wiped her mouth with her napkin. "Let's make some more tea. We agreed we need to clear the air."

"Hmm. Yes, we did." They carried the remains of dinner into the kitchen. "You cooked. I'll clean up. While Casey wiped the table and tidied up the dining room, Mica washed the dishes. "Go on in and sit down. I'll bring the tea in as soon as the water boils." The kettle whistled as she dried the last plate.

Mica found Casey at the dining table, chin propped on both hands. She placed the tea on the placemat and sat down. "There ya go. The magic elixir that cures everything that ails you. What's troubling you?"

"I don't know. Things between us have been...different. We haven't been hanging out like we used to."

"Hmm." Mica's eyes narrowed. "You've been busy."

"I had a lot to do for Grams, to get the place set up for Millie to move in. I'll not bore you with the list. I don't know how you noticed, you've been unavailable," Casey snapped. Silence hung in the air between them, neither ready or willing to move the conversation forward.

"I'm sorry." Casey chewed her lip. "I don't want to fight. That's the last thing I intended tonight."

"Why do you sound so angry then?"

There was silence but for the sound of Casey's foot tapping on the floor and the clock ticking on the wall. Casey scratched her cheek. "I've been doing a lot of thinking. It's not really you I'm angry with. I'm mostly pissed at myself." Casey's eyes filled. "I've been jealous."

"I told you that you have nothing to worry about in that regard." Mica's eyes softened.

"The thing that caused the biggest change between us was the massage. We never talked about that night. I feel like I ruined something special we had. Mica, I miss us. I wanted you to know that. I know it was my fault. I'm sorry."

It was Mica's turn to chew her lip. "Okay." Mica gave a quick shake of her head. "No, I think we both bear some responsibility. I've thought about it dozens of times and still can't figure out what happened. How many times have we touched each other in the past and felt nothing? Clearly, we were feeling something that night. And that kiss on New Year's Eve. It was barely more than a peck. Still, it felt like three seconds of magic. Maybe we need to be more honest with each other about what exactly is going on."

Although Casey nodded her head in agreement, she didn't reply.

"And here we are back at the same spot as usual." Mica drummed her fingers on the table. "Neither of us is ready to take a risk and talk about our feelings."

"I'd be willing to do that if only I could figure out what those feelings are." Casey raised a shoulder in a half shrug. "How about you?"

"Okay, I'll tell you what I'm feeling. At least I'll try. Sometimes I feel like we have this *thing* going on between us."

"Thing?"

"Yeah, a *thing*. I don't even know how to describe it...not exactly approach/avoidance or push/pull..." Mica blew out a breath and ran her fingers through her hair. "I mean you've always, always, always said you'd *never* get involved with a friend after what's her name."

"Jennifer?"

"Right...Jennifer. Yet, over the past five or six months...our friendship felt different. We were together all the time. Working with each other all day and, until recently, spending almost every night and weekend with each other."

Casey nodded. "I know. You're right. I never tire of being with you. If we don't spend time with each other after work, I miss you."

"Yes. I feel the same way." Mica could feel the vibration from the rapid motion of Casey's leg as it shook against the table. Avoiding Casey's eyes, she studied the pattern on the teaspoon trying to organize her thoughts. After inhaling a deep breath, Mica licked her lips and raised her head. "Despite what you've said about friends and lovers being mutually exclusive, there are times that I feel there's a glimmer of that *thing* between us. Some nights I can feel it. You're right there, only a kiss away. During those times, I believe...no, I'm certain that you've finally let go of that old conviction. I'm ready to reach for it...to reach for you, and suddenly, like a wisp of smoke in a breeze, that *thing* is gone. I'm left to wonder if that moment was real, or if it's only me who wishes it were."

"No. There are times I want it all too. With you." Tears threatened to spill from Casey's eyes. "And then...I get scared and hurt you. I'm sorry I'm such a coward." Two large tears rolled down Casey's cheeks.

"Please, don't cry." Mica stood. She took Casey by the hands and pulled until she rose to her feet. "Come here." Wrapping Casey in her arms, she squeezed until Casey hugged her back.

"I'm afraid, Mica. I don't want to hurt you. I don't want to lose your friendship or ruin our business relationship. I'm not sure I can..."

"Shh." Mica leaned back and waited for Casey to meet her eyes. "We've made progress. We've admitted that we'd both like more." She felt Casey tense and stepped back, joining their hands. "We both want the same things. How we go about that is the problem."

"Oh, Mica, what if..."

"Shh." Mica stepped in, wrapped Casey in her arms, and waited for her to relax again. Casey's shoulders finally lowered so they no longer looked as though they were suspended from her ear lobes. She rested her hands on Mica's hips.

"I fear saying this because I don't want you to run away from me again. I care for you very deeply, Casey." Mica leaned back enough that she could look into Casey's eyes. "If that elusive something more ever happens between us, I swear to you, no matter what, you'll *always* be my friend and business partner." She released her right hand and used it to cross her heart. "I can say that with confidence because I know with one hundred percent certainty that you'd never hurt me intentionally. I'm willing to take that risk with you."

Casey opened her mouth to speak, and Mica stopped her with a light touch of her fingers. Mica shook her head. "Not yet. Don't say anything. Let all this settle. Okay?" She dropped her hand.

"Yes." Casey smiled and placed her palm against Mica's cheek.

"We good?" Mica covered Casey's hand with her own.

Casey nodded. "At least until you run off with Eden." There was a twinkle in Casey's eyes.

"What? How'd you know?" Mica stepped back. She kept a straight face until Casey smacked her. "Hey, you have to admit that Eden's really hot. You might have to worry if she played for our team, which she doesn't. Her boyfriend is about six foot five and as gorgeous as she is."

"Hmm. I'm hopeful that her being straight isn't the only reason you haven't tossed me aside and never looked back."

"You're awfully possessive for someone who's been unwilling to be my girlfriend."

"Well, that's probably true." Casey chuckled and looked toward the box on the hutch. "I got you a present. Now, with that attitude, I'm not sure I want to give it to you."

"A present?" Mica looked up toward the bedroom door.

"Stop."

Mica grinned and wiggled her left eyebrow.

"I've never understood how you could do that."

"Do what?"

"Wiggle one eyebrow." Casey's finger, as light as a butterfly across Mica's eyebrow, elicited a sharp intake of breath.

Mica exhaled and stepped back. "It's one of my innumerable talents."

Casey rolled her eyes and reached for the box on the hutch. "Here, hurry up and open it. I can't wait to see your reaction."

Mica tore the envelope and read the card.

For the friend I love the most.

Inside the box, Mica found airline tickets, a brochure, and reservations for the Match Me vacation. "Holy crap! How'd you manage this? Nell won this trip." Mica paled and nearly broke out in a sweat. "Oh no. I don't have to go with Nell, do I?" Fright white turned to angry red in a matter of seconds.

"No, no...calm down before steam comes out of your ears." Casey held up both hands in front of her. "I bought it from her. You wanted it so badly, and I wanted you to have it."

"Oh, Case, that's really sweet. What did she say when you called her?"

"She told me she hadn't met anyone yet, and she was more than willing to sell it. I think she was genuinely happy about it. Her response was, 'OMG, epic.' That means happy, right?"

Mica chuckled and kissed Casey on the cheek. She'd given a brief consideration to a peck on the lips, but didn't want to ruin their newly found détente.

"According to the brochure, you're free to take any guest you want."

"Really?" Mica's eyes narrowed as she thumbed through the brochure. "Hmm. Look here." She pointed to the fine print. "Did you know this?"

"What?"

Mica read aloud. *"This is a romantic island rental perfect for a couple. There is no electricity on the island.* Hmm...I guess candlelight is romantic. The first part of the vacation sounds posh, though. It's a resort with a sandy beach, sun, and those drinks with the little umbrellas."

"Sounds nice. I hope you'll have fun." Casey picked up their cups and started for the kitchen.

"Oh no. You're coming with me. Especially now."

Casey's voice drifted in from the kitchen. "We can't both leave Fit As A Fiddle at the same time."

"Come on. We talked about this when we signed up."

"I know." Casey returned to the dining area. "That was totally theoretical."

"We can do it, Case, especially with Eden there. She's up to speed already, and by the time we leave she'll be fine. By cutting back on new clients for a couple weeks, we can hire consultants to fill in as needed. I'll arrange all that. By the time we leave, Grams and Millie will be back. Hell, they could run the place themselves. Please..."

By the time Mica was ready to leave for home, she'd convinced Casey they'd have a great time and the business would survive without them. "It's getting late, I'd better go." Mica slipped her arm into her coat and started for the door. She could feel Casey slowing her pace behind her. Mica turned around, leaned her back against the door, and held out her hands. She could see the pulse pounding in Casey's neck. From the wide-eyed look on her face, Mica knew it wasn't from excitement at the idea of kissing her.

"Give me your hands. I won't bite. Promise."

One shaking hand reached out. The other trailed a few seconds later, after Casey wiped it on her jeans.

Mica tugged Casey gently closer. "How many times in the past twenty or so years do you think we've touched or hugged each other? Why should tonight be any different? Just because we admitted that we've had moments of attraction doesn't mean anything has to change right away—or ever, for that matter."

"Really?"

Mica dropped Casey's hands and smiled at the look of relief that sprinted across Casey's face. "Really." Mica's voice softened to a near whisper. "I'd love it if it did, though. Sex, Casey. Do you remember that?" She wet her lips. "Not just sex. An intimacy that means something both physically and emotionally." Mica watched Casey put a hand against the wall and close her eyes, her breath coming softly through slightly parted lips. A few heartbeats later, Mica continued. "I'm talking about touch that creates pleasure for both the receiver and the giver. Every touch leaves a trail of fiery goosebumps."

Casey's eyes snapped open and she took a step backward. "Oh, God! Who are you and what have you done with my friend, Mica?"

"Well, I've dreamed of hearing you yell 'oh God,' only not like that." Mica laughed. She stepped forward and gave Casey a quick hug. "We're going to be fine. Let's worry about getting ready for the trip. Everything else will take care of itself."

CHAPTER TWENTY

CASEY TALKED TO HERSELF all the way to work the next morning. The closer she got, the wetter her underarms became. The red light was not long enough to allow her to massage away the headache between her brows. A quick glance revealed a haggard stranger staring back from the rearview mirror.

Casey parked beside Mica's car. *She must have an early client.* Her hand paused on the handle of the gym's familiar front door. *Oh God, how can I face Mica?* Casey pushed through the entrance with the same pit in her stomach usually reserved for her annual gynecological visit and hurried to the back. She left her coat in the office and dropped her lunch in the fridge. Chewing her lip, she made her way down the hallway to the gym.

Mica looked up and tossed her a wave and a grin from across the therapy room. The sudden release of Casey's tense muscles left her as limp as a wet noodle. She flopped into Trish's chair, fearing her legs might not support her any longer. *Huh. The world didn't come to an end. Mica is still Mica. Maybe we really are okay.*

***

The week flew by. By Saturday, they realized how much help Grams and Millie were with the corner group. Mica and Casey were the last two remaining in the building and were getting ready to close for the day. Casey shrugged into her coat. "I think Eden has proven herself to be very capable. I'm glad we hired her."

"Me too. I think it was a good decision. What are you doing tomorrow?" Mica took the coat Casey extended to her.

"I thought I'd do some shopping for the trip. Coming?"

"I wouldn't miss it. Do I get to watch you try on bikinis?" Mica placed her hand on her heart and made a quick beating motion.

"You're impossible." A red flush crept up from Casey's neck to her hairline.

Encouraged that Casey was still chuckling, Mica led the way out to their cars. She paused, her hand on the door handle, to look at her friend over the roof of the car. "Would you like to go out with me tonight? Maybe we could grab a pizza and see a movie?"

"Go out?"

"Yes. Go out. Like on a date."

Casey's hand flew to her neck and froze. She stood still as a deer in the headlights. Her unblinking eyes stared straight ahead while Mica held her breath and said a silent prayer.

"Okay. Where to?"

"Nicola's? We can pick a movie while we eat."

The response came in an unsteady voice. "Okay."

Mica nodded her head. "Good. If this is going to be a date, then I think you should come with me. We can leave your car here for now. I'll drive you back to it later."

Mica thought she might have to go over and take the immobile woman by the hand to get her to move. Eventually, with a classic case of slow feet, Casey came around the front of the car. They met, and Mica walked her to the passenger side and opened the door. Casey got in and Mica hurried around to the driver's side. Casey didn't say anything for the first several minutes, so Mica risked teasing her.

"So, you from around here?"

Casey burst into laughter. "You're an idiot."

"Could be, but I'm your idiot." She reached over and took Casey's hand.

At their favorite pizza joint, they couldn't agree on red or white, so they got individual pies and a small side salad each. Mica wrinkled her nose at the anchovies on Casey's pizza. "Are you trying to assure that I'll not want to kiss you good night?"

Casey's eyebrows shot up, nearly to her hairline. "What? You kiss on a first date?"

"If I really like the person. However, those hairy little fish you ordered on your pizza, are a definite kiss deterrent."

Casey laughed. "If that's all it takes to discourage you..." Her voice trailed off.

They both reached for the check. Mica gently pulled it away. "I asked you out, remember? That means I pay."

"Next time, it's my turn."

"Oooh progress. I can't wait to see where you take me on our second date."

They had the waitress box up the leftover pizza for lunch the next day. They bought tickets for what must be the tenth remake of *Murder On The Orient Express* and climbed up to their seats in the last row at the top of the stairs, then settled in to enjoy the show.

Casey looked around them. There was another couple on the other side of the theater in their same row. "It's a good thing this movie doesn't appeal to a younger audience, or we'd be up here with all the kids who come to the movies to neck."

Mica grinned. "I see you figured out my plan."

Mica noted that after Casey rolled her eyes, she sat with her hands folded in her lap. As the opening credits began, Mica felt Casey's hand slip onto the shared armrest, snake behind her elbow and slide down her arm, coming to rest on Mica's forearm. Mica closed her eyes and allowed the warmth to spread down her torso and settle between her legs. She sucked in her bottom lip and turned her head to glance over at Casey. Their eyes met, and when Casey squeezed her arm, Mica slid it back to join their hands.

"I figured it was safe to do that because I ate the anchovies," Casey whispered.

Mica grinned. *Maybe playing it a little hard to get for a month or so worked.* She drew Casey's hand to her lips and placed a quick kiss there. "That'll hold me until you're ready for more."

On the ride home, Mica reached for Casey's hand. She drew it flat against her own thigh and covered Casey's hand with her own. "This is nice. Does it feel okay to you?"

"It's different. I feel, um…" Casey tipped her head to the side. "I feel like a schoolgirl doing something I'm not sure I'm supposed to be doing. It feels a little naughty."

"No, about six inches higher would be naughty. This is definitely nice." Mica laughed and was pleased to see a smile on Casey's face as well.

"Mica, how can you be so sure you want whatever this is to progress to naughty? Every time I even think about it, I'm terrified that the next time I see you, things will be different between us."

"Have I ever lied to you?"

"Not that I'm aware of. You are always truthful and honest, not only with me, with others too."

"Then, why can't you believe what I've promised you? I'm not going to change. You keep thinking that for some reason our becoming a couple won't work out. You are looking at the glass half empty."

"I know."

"If you're right, the worst that can happen is that we may have a few awkward weeks. Eventually, we'll straighten it all out. Can't you trust in us...believe in us?"

"I'm trying. After Jennifer, I always swore..."

"Forget her. I'm not her. I'm the person you've known most of your life, your friend, your business partner, and I want to be your lover. Think of how great we could have it. We could have it all." Mica pulled up next to Casey's car.

Casey pulled her hand away and released her seat belt. "I know in my heart what you're saying is true. Be patient with me. I'm trying." She reached for the door handle, then turned and reached across Mica to cup her cheek.

Mica wrapped her hand around Casey's and placed a soft kiss in her palm. As Casey opened her mouth to speak, Mica interrupted. "Please, don't say anything. In the past, you've always made a serious moment evaporate with a flip comment. Don't do that this time, please."

Casey shook her head and leaned over. She placed a quick kiss on Mica's cheek. "Thank you for tonight. I had a very nice time."

"Me too. I'll pick you up around nine thirty, to go shopping." Seeing the look of horror cross Casey's face, Mica laughed. "Ten?"

"Ten, if you'll treat me to breakfast."

"Done." Mica waited for Casey to settle in her car and crank the engine to life. She followed her for several blocks, until they turned in different directions, heading for their individual homes.

***

Mica texted that she was on her way over, so as she pulled up in front of the house, Casey came trotting out. Mica handed her a bag with a blueberry muffin in it. "I've been up since six. I gave up waiting for breakfast around eight. There's a container of tea in the cup holder."

"This is your idea of a date for breakfast? I may have to rethink this girlfriend idea." Casey inhaled the aroma of the muffin.

"Don't I even get points for getting you perfectly sweetened tea and the blueberry muffin you love?" Mica glanced at the expression on Casey's face. "I guess from that curled lip, the answer is no." Mica made the turn toward the mall. "Will it help if I tell you I was so excited about watching you try on a bathing suit, I didn't want to waste time with a

100

proper, sit down breakfast?"

As they made the rounds of the stores, their companionship was easy. Casey was buying new underwear. "What's wrong with your old underwear?" Mica asked.

"Remember the baggage handlers and customs people? I don't want them seeing my old stuff."

Mica pouted. "Oh, I thought it was for me."

"For you? You told me I wouldn't need clothes."

"No, I said, all you'll need is a bathing suit."

"Why will we need suits on an island with only the two of us?" Casey grazed the corner of Mica's mouth with her fingertip. She glanced around to be sure no one could hear her. "I've always loved the cleft in your chin. It's very sexy, you know."

Mica forced her mouth closed and wondered if Casey had always been a flirt. It was a characteristic she'd never noticed before. However, it was one she most definitely liked.

"Come on, let's go pick out swimsuits."

Mica's hopes to see Casey try on the suit were dashed the minute she noted that the store had individual dressing rooms. They picked out two suits each, thinking that one could be drying while they wore the other.

Loaded with bags, they turned toward the exit. "Oh, one more stop." Casey led the way to the sporting goods store.

"What do you want here?"

"We're going to a tiny island...they describe it as rustic. I'm not drinking the water. I want to get a straw-type water filter and some purification tablets. We also need one of those lightweight tents for the beach. I looked up the island, and there's no vegetation near the water. We need shade, or we'll turn into lobsters. I did some research, and this tent weighs only a few ounces and folds up to almost nothing." Casey let her eyes travel the length of Mica's body. "You'll need it, especially if you're planning to be sans suit."

Mica's mouth dropped open. Almost instantly her shock was replaced by a sly and hopeful grin.

"I also always travel with a little first aid kit, sewing kit, a flashlight, a lighter, a couple of good quality emergency blankets, and some packs of those little tissues. They're handy in places without TP."

Casey looked through a display of bags for one that would hold all her purchases and finally settled on a small, nylon sack with handy pouches sewn in the sides. She plucked her choice from the selection and inspected it carefully. A quick nod indicated her confidence that she could fit everything she bought inside by using the handy pockets and nesting the larger items in the middle.

The clerk arranged the items for checkout. "Where are you headed?"

Casey disclosed their destination. "Oh, then you'll definitely need to bring sunscreen, bug spray, and an after-bite medication to help with the itch if the bug spray fails you." He wrote the name of a gel that was good for soothing sunburn. "It's also good for long-term relief of mosquito and sand flea bites. You can get it at any of the chain drugstores."

As the man turned away to ring up their purchases, Mica leaned over and whispered. "Now I'm not so sure I want to go. A deserted tropical island sounds a lot less romantic if I'm going to be eaten alive."

"It'll be fine. We'll be prepared for every problem."

They stopped at a small craft fair in the mall lobby. One booth was selling Turks head bracelets. Casey chose simple white cotton, and Mica chose a blue and white one. The crafter helped them select the proper sizes for their sailor's bracelets. "These are so neat. I love mine." Mica rotated hers on her wrist. "I can't see where it begins or where it ends."

"Think of it like our friendship." Casey squeezed Mica's hand. They gathered their purchases and headed for the car. "It's almost dark already. Where did the day go?"

They stopped for a quick meal, before heading for Casey's home, where Mica helped Casey carry all her purchases inside. Casey bent over and picked up Simon to quell his noisy complaints about being alone all day. "You want to watch some tube?"

Mica sighed and scratched the cat's soft ear. "I don't think I can stay awake. You know how much I love shopping."

"I'm crushed. I thought we had fun."

"We did. I always enjoy spending time with you. It would have been more fun if we were doing something other than shopping, like having a root canal."

"You're impossible." Casey shook her head.

"It's a work day tomorrow, and I want to get these new things washed. We only have one more weekend and a few days after that before we leave." Mica took Casey's hand and led her toward the front door. "I'm not sure if I'm more excited or nervous about our trip." She turned around at the door and opened her arms. "Think I can get a hug tonight?"

Casey took a step forward, remaining a foot away. "Are we sure we want to do this? You know, to risk everything we already have?"

"I am. Are you? The thought of falling in love with you makes me feel like the last piece of a puzzle is sliding into place. Take a chance with me, Casey."

Casey stepped into Mica's embrace. They exhaled a mutual sigh as their bodies met. Before Mica tightened her grip, Casey gave her a quick kiss on the lips and stepped back. "You're tired, remember?"

Mica reached for Casey and reversed their positions. "Let's see if I can convince you I'm awake enough for us to enjoy this." She brought her mouth a half inch away from the lips she craved to taste...and waited. She could feel Casey's breath mingling with her own.

Time stood still, until Casey closed the gap between their mouths. The kiss was gentle and lingering. Mica pulled back to allow them to breathe. Casey slid her hand behind Mica's neck and tugged. Their lips came together, and mutual need pushed them to open for each other as their tongues explored. Mica struggled with her desire, eventually managing to pull away. She rested her forehead against Casey's.

"I'd better go, even though I don't want to."

Casey straightened. "Are you sorry we did that?"

"God no! I regret that we didn't do that years ago. Why didn't you tell me you could kiss like that?"

Casey grabbed Mica's coat and pulled her back against her. "Do it again."

Mica moaned, "Oh God!" as she slipped her hands under Casey's shirt and slid them up her back, never breaking the contact of their mouths. Mica's tongue demanded entry, exploring until Casey broke the kiss.

"I'm sorry. I lost control." Mica hoped her eyes showed her concern.

"Stop. I'm fine. There were two people involved, and I was enjoying myself. Maybe we need to let all this settle a bit, though."

"I know. Patience." Mica kissed Casey on the nose. "I'll see you in the morning." She opened the door. "You okay?"

"I'm fine. See you tomorrow."

***

Mica had a fitful night. She was one hundred percent certain there was not one position the human body could assume that she had not tried in her effort to sleep. She gave up early, showered, and ate a protein bar on the way to work. Casey's car was the only one in the parking lot. *Good, we're alone for a little while.* Her mind raced. *How will Casey react?* As she passed the door to the break room, an arm suddenly reached out and grabbed her by the collar. She was pulled into the room and pressed against the wall.

Casey's mouth was everywhere, kissing her lips, her eyes, nuzzling into her neck. She explored upwards with her tongue to taste Mica's skin, eventually pausing to trace the intricacies of Mica's ear before returning to her mouth and searing her lips with a kiss. "I couldn't get you out of my mind last night. All I could think of was kissing you again and feeling your hands on me."

"You're making me crazy." Mica murmured before she plunged her tongue deep into Casey's mouth. Mica's moan brought them to their senses. They heard the front door open and Trish call for them.

"We're in the back. Be right out." Casey groaned as she pulled away.

Mica steadied herself against the door jamb and looked at Casey. Noticing the dark circles under Casey's eyes pulled a chuckle from Mica. "You look as exhausted as I do." Mica sighed and moistened her lips, tasting the flavor of Casey's lipstick left there from their kisses.

While Mica adjusted her clothing, Casey tried to wipe away her smeared lipstick. Mica took the tissue from Casey's trembling fingers. "Here, let me." She waited for Casey to stick out her tongue to moisten the tissue before she carefully dabbed away the smudges. "Perfect." She stepped away seconds before Trish entered the break room to put her lunch in the fridge.

"Good morning. You're both in early." Trish stopped and studied their faces. "You two are working too hard. You both look like you hardly slept a wink." Continuing on her way toward the fridge, Trish glanced back at Mica. "When did you start wearing lipstick? I like it."

Mica bulged her eyes at Casey, who was biting her lip in an effort not to laugh. "We'll be in our office, Trish." Retreating to their shared space, they each sat at their own desks, in an unspoken agreement that they needed to keep a safe distance from each other.

Casey looked at Mica and licked her lips. "I nearly drove to your house at 3:48 this morning, I wanted you so much."

"Wish you had." Mica grinned. "I was certainly awake. Why didn't you?"

"Because I knew we wouldn't stop at kissing, and I don't want to rush through what I know is going to be something very special."

"See, while you're saying things so nicely, about the only thought I have running through my mind is 'I can't ever remember being this horny, or this hot for anyone.'" Mica closed her legs and swiveled her chair back and forth a few times.

"Stop that!"

"What?" Mica pulled her most innocent look.

"You know what I mean." Casey gestured with her head in the general direction of Mica's crotch. "Did you take care of things yourself this morning?"

"I won't deny I was tempted. For some reason, I wanted the experience to be *with* you, not about you. We've waited this long. I'd kind of like to wait for our trip. It'll feel like a honeymoon."

"I'm glad we're on the same page. The first time we make love, I don't want it to be rushed." Casey leaned her cheek against her closed fist and rested her elbow on her desk. She yawned twice. "How am I going to make it through today?"

"One step at a time. Come on, I'm sure our patients are about due."

AJ Adaire

CHAPTER TWENTY-ONE

FINISHED WITH HER SANDWICH, Mica began unwrapping her cream filled chocolate cupcakes. "The clients love Eden, not only for her skills but for her kindness. She's always upbeat and ready to laugh."

Casey watched as Mica licked cream from her lips. "Eden and Trish have really hit it off. I love their frequent banter. They keep us laughing right along with them. The fact that they get along so well together has helped me begin to anticipate our vacation with excitement."

"Eden got her friend, Sylvia, to help fill in while we're gone." One of the therapists where Eden worked before had decided she wasn't going to enjoy the new owner. Eden brought her in to meet Casey and Mica, who liked her immediately.

"Thanks, Mica, for driving to the airport last night to pick up Grams and Millie. I had fun listening to the two of them go on and on about their trip. They had a ball on their cruise. I bet Grams still hasn't stopped talking about how she won the thousand-dollar bingo jackpot. They really enjoyed the musical shows, too. I'm so glad they went."

"Me too. Are you packed yet?" Mica took a bite of her cupcake and licked the cream filling from her finger. "What's the matter? You're staring."

"Nothing's wrong. I just noticed you licking your finger. I don't think I've ever seen you do that before."

"I'm sure I do it all the time. Maybe you've never paid attention before." Mica winked and folded up her cupcake wrappings and stuffed them into her brown bag.

"To answer your question about packing, nothing is in the suitcases yet. I've started gathering things together that I know I'll need."

Mica frowned. "How many suitcases are you bringing? Remember, all we need are swimsuits."

"One and a carry-on. I have extra room in my carry-on for some of your essentials just in case they lose our luggage."

Casey drifted between her private thoughts and the soliloquy Mica had launched into about too many belongings and lugging things with them.

"...travel light. Nothing but..."

Casey's eyes narrowed, as she thought back over the past week. *Conversations have been our normal, fun and light banter. She's been my old friend, except that I feel like a high school boy with his first crush. Oh God! Why can't I get the things I want to do to her out of my mind?*

Casey tried to focus on what Mica was saying. She heard "Easier to change planes if..." Instead, the words Mica said to her that night she spoke of intimacy and *trails of fiery goosebumps* drowned out the rest of what she said.

***

Saturday afternoon, she and Mica had taken Grams and Millie food shopping and helped them stock up on everything they could imagine needing. Mica drove Casey home, and after a quick make out session in the car, she begged off coming in. "If we want to keep our promise to wait for our vacation, you need to let me go home. Besides, I have to clean and pack."

"Clean? Why? It'll be dirty again by the time we get back home." Casey snuggled against Mica's neck. "I was so stupid. I apologize for not wanting us to be more than friends. If not for me, we'd probably be curled up in bed together right now." Her hand slipped up under Mica's shirt. The nipple she found grew firm the second she touched it. Mica moaned. "Umm. Isn't this nice." Casey rolled her palm over Mica's breast, each enjoying the sensation.

"You're not playing fair," Mica whispered. Her tongue traced the contours of Casey's ear.

"Um hm. You want me to stop?"

Mica covered Casey's hand with her own. "No. Leave your hand there. If you keep moving, you're going to make me come just from you playing with my breast. As much as I love it when you touch me, I think I'd better go right now, or I'm going to break my promise."

They both sighed.

"I know." Casey sat up. "Are we being stupid by waiting?"

Mica leaned over and kissed Casey. "No. I think it's been a good thing. Each day we've waited, I've seen you grow surer of your decision to trust us. Surer that we'll be good as a couple."

"Yes. That's true." Casey touched Mica's cheek. Her eyes softened. "I think that the first time you really kissed me, I knew it was right. Each day, my confidence in us has grown at least as much as my need for you." Casey reached for the door handle. "Thank you for being patient. I promise it'll be worth it."

"I have no doubts." Their parting kiss was more sweet than filled with lust.

***

Casey slept late on her last Sunday at home before she and Mica were scheduled to leave on their trip. Still in her pajamas, she cleaned the house, took out the trash, and organized food and supplies she'd bought for Simon. It took another fifteen minutes to type up instructions to her cat sitter on how and when to feed, play, scoop, and care for her fur baby. She added contact information for the vet and directions on how to get there. Following her shower, she dressed in warm-ups and shuffled downstairs to put the teakettle on.

While waiting for the water to boil, she flopped down at her kitchen table and rubbed her eyes. The lottery ticket, casually tossed there the previous week, caught her attention. The shrill whistle indicated that her water was ready. Tea in one hand and a quarter from her change jar in the other, she returned to the table. Opening her napkin in front of her, she placed the ticket in the center and started scratching. There were nine boxes displayed. The instructions said that three like amounts were required to win. Using the quarter to remove the covering from the first three boxes revealed prizes of one, five, and five hundred dollars. The next three boxes showed one dollar, a free ticket, and another five-hundred-dollar spot. "Oooh! Maybe I'll win the five hundred bucks." The first box in the last column showed five million dollars. Casey's pulse stepped up its pace as she scratched the second spot to reveal a five, but her spirits dropped when she scratched off the rest of the covering to reveal it was five million, not five hundred. Drawing out the suspense, she scratched a tiny portion of the corner of the final square. It was a five. Taking a deep breath, Casey dragged the quarter across the last covered area to reveal the amount in the final square. *Five million. Damn.* About to tear the lottery card in half, reality hit her. The bottom three amounts matched.

Five million, five million, five million.

"It can't be." With shaking hands, she reread the rules and looked again. "Oh my God!" She gasped and clasped it to her chest.

Following one more scrutiny of the amounts, Casey jumped to her feet. Her behavior mimicked one of those ducks in the shooting arcade. Her feet were anchored to the floor, as her body angled toward the hutch, then reversed direction to the kitchen junk drawer, then back to the hutch again. Her eyes darted around the room. *Where do I put the thing?* "Oh…I'd better sign it." After trying several hiding places, she tucked the ticket in her bra and grabbed the vodka from the living room. Back in the kitchen, Casey paused as she unscrewed the cap on the bottle. *What the hell, it must be five o'clock somewhere and this is a very special occasion.* She poured herself three fingers of the clear liquid, added a splash of orange juice, and drank it down in a few gulps. The fire burned its way through her belly and warmed her extremities.

Plopping down at the kitchen table, she pulled the ticket from her bra and checked it again. Still-shaky fingers tapped out the phone numbers, in turn, of her accountant, her lawyer, and her investment advisor. Upon hearing her news, they all agreed to cancel their morning appointments, enabling them to see her at nine the next morning. Her last call was to Trish to ask her to reschedule her appointments.

***

"Hey! Where were you yesterday?" Mica checked her watch, happy she had a few minutes between patients.

"I felt a little strange on Sunday evening, and I had a hard time getting to sleep. Yesterday morning, I still didn't feel, uh…quite like myself." Casey crossed her fingers behind her back.

"Trish told me you'd called in and asked her to reschedule your appointments. I tried to call you…"

"I had the phone turned off. I thought I'd better take it easy in case I was coming down with something." Although Casey hated telling the white lie to Mica, she'd decided to wait to tell her about the win until they were on the trip. There was an idea she wanted to explore with Mica before revealing the news.

CHAPTER TWENTY-TWO

THE DAY BEFORE THEIR departure, Casey caught up with Mica in their office during a few minutes of free time between patients. "Have you been watching the weather?"

"Yes."

"They're predicting ice and snow. Maybe we should call a limo service to take us to the airport."

Using her forefinger, Mica rubbed the furrow between Casey's eyes in an effort to smooth away the concern. "Relax. My car has all-wheel drive. We'll be fine if we give ourselves some extra time."

"I don't know why I seem to have such an ominous feeling about this trip."

"Because you were born a worrywart who stresses about everything." Mica wrapped her arms around Casey and pulled her close. "It makes my life ever so much easier. I don't have to have a care about anything."

"What a pair we are."

"The only concern I have is that you'll change your mind about us." Mica leaned back and searched Casey's face.

"No. You wore me down and convinced me you were worth the risk. I've never known you to lie to me."

"Hmm...well, there was the one time I told you I thought Haley was a good person and you should date her."

"She was a good person. Good for someone other than me."

They both laughed. Mica leaned in and placed a gentle kiss on Casey's lips.

"I have to get back out there. Don't forget we have an appointment after lunch for our spray tans." They'd both taken the afternoon off to finish up preparations for their trip. "We'll leave right after we meet with the staff to make sure they're ready for us to be gone."

Oh, they're ready for us to be gone all right. Mica bit her tongue. Casey had written reams of instructions and cautions for Eden and the rest of the crew that she'd distributed at the staff meeting the week before. Only once had Mica detected an eye roll Eden shared with Trish, as Casey reviewed all the points she considered critical. Casey had also arranged for Eden to cat sit for Simon. The list of instructions for him made the ones she'd shared at the meeting seem paltry by comparison.

They finally got away from their office with barely enough time to make it to the tanning studio. "Oh! We need to go back. I forgot to tell Trish— "

"You can always send her a message. You're only a text away. Let them handle it." She reached over and took Casey's hand and drew it to her lips.

"You're right. I'm micromanaging a very competent group of people. I hope they don't think I'm worried they can't handle things in our absence."

"What would possibly give them that idea?"

"You're being sarcastic, aren't you?"

"Who, me? I don't even know the meaning of that word." Mica smirked before squeezing Casey's hand. "Everything will be fine. They love you and know you're nervous. Now, please, relax and remember that there's nothing that can go wrong while we're away that we can't fix upon our return."

Casey shrugged one shoulder. "I know you're right."

"Good. I'm always right." She grinned. "Remember that."

"You may not always be right, but you're never in doubt."

***

"How dark do you want me to make you?" The tanning specialist pushed a color chart toward each of them. Mica, one of those naturally golden people, pointed to a swatch a couple shades darker than her natural skin tone. Casey watched Mica's selection and said, "I want to be as tan as she'll be."

The consultant arched an eyebrow. "You do realize that she has a bit of a head start."

"Can you do it?"

The technician assigned to Casey nodded. "Sure. Let me show you the dressing room."

They followed her down a long, dimly lit hallway to the women's tiny changing area. She showed them each a locker and explained how the lock worked. "There are items inside for you to wear. Pick one for your use while you're here. Take everything off and put on the paper underwear, robe, and slippers. Someone will be back to show you to the booth in a few minutes." The woman with the stiff, businesslike attitude that bordered on standoffish hurried down the hallway.

"Is the heat off in here or was the cold emanating from ice woman?" Mica shrugged her shoulders and rubbed her hands up and down her arms, feigning a chill.

Casey smirked. "She's probably busy."

"How busy can she be?" Mica glanced around. "We're the only two customers in the entire place. I hope that doesn't indicate how skilled they are."

"Come on. Let's get ready. Are there private dressing booths?"

"I don't see any. Seriously? This is it. They have ten lockers in this room and it's nearly full with only two of us in here."

Of course, they'd seen each other in various stages of undress over the years. As the realization dawned that they'd have to get completely naked in front of each other, their eyes met, and both sets of eyebrows rose toward their hairlines.

"We can play this one of two ways." Mica leaned against the locker. "I can turn around and give you privacy, or we can simply enjoy the experience." She reached for her sweatshirt and teased the hem up a few inches to expose her stomach. Casey's audible intake of breath answered for her. Mica stripped the shirt the rest of the way over her head to reveal her breasts.

"No bra?" Casey reached out and placed a finger in the hollow where Mica's collarbones met and slowly traced downward toward the cleavage between her breasts.

Mica stepped back a few inches and raised her finger, shaking it slowly left and right like a scolding teacher. "Think about where we are." She stuck her thumbs in the waistband of her sweatpants and pulled down on one side to reveal more skin. "I read on the internet that it isn't recommended to wear a bra after being sprayed, so I decided not to wear one here. One less thing to keep track of." She tugged on the other side of her sweats to lower them to just above her neatly trimmed hairline.

Mica's eyes darkened, and Casey licked her lips in anticipation. With a quick motion, Mica pushed, and her sweatpants hit the floor. Casey blushed as her eyes caressed every inch of Mica's naked body. Despite the fact they were nearly a foot apart, she could feel the heat reflecting off Mica's body.

"You're beautiful. How could I have been so stupid all these years...me and my never-get-involved-with-a-friend principle?"

"You were saving the best for last." Mica's eyes glinted. "Your turn." Mica cocked an eyebrow and leaned back against the door, waiting.

Casey pulled on the tie holding up her loose sweatpants and stripped them off, along with her underwear. She stepped out of the pants before reaching for the first button below the collar of her shirt. One by one, she released them until her top hung slightly open, allowing Mica a glimpse of skin beneath. She shrugged out of the garment and smiled. "Unlike you, I wore a bra. I could use some help releasing it."

Mica reached around Casey and pulled her closer, making quick work of the hooks until the last barrier restricting their skin-on-skin contact fell away. She stripped it off and pulled Casey against her. Their lips met in a searing kiss, as Casey's hands slid up Mica's body. Her lips parted, as Mica's tongue sought entrance. "Oh my God, somebody's coming." Casey stepped away and turned her back, hurrying the few feet to the locker seconds before a sharp knock sounded.

"You two ready?" The chilly voice of the unfriendly staffer boomed from the other side of the closed door.

"Almost. Give us a couple more minutes, please." Mica winked at Casey.

Casey was still beet red. She grabbed the robe from her locker, a close relative of those used during a mammogram, and picked up the spa provided paper panties. She glanced back over her shoulder. "Come on, we have to get ready." She put her hand to her chest and blew out a quick breath through pursed lips. "That was close. She nearly caught us."

"Obviously, our host, in addition to being inhospitable, has an astonishingly bad sense of timing." Unmindful or uncaring about the fact that she was completely naked, Mica crossed the room and opened her locker. She slipped the crinkly robe on and plucked the paper panties from their plastic wrap. "These are interesting." She held up the triangle of paper barely larger than an English muffin that narrowed to a one-inch wide strip. The band of paper was suspended from a thin rubber thread. "Good God! I think they cut these stretchy things from their file folders. They could have simply given us a Band-Aid and called it good."

Casey couldn't keep her eyes off the slim opening in Mica's robe. "Aren't you the least bit bothered that she nearly caught us necking naked?"

"Nearly necking naked...is that an alliteration?" Mica's eyes sparkled with mischief. "No, I wasn't afraid. I was leaning against the door for a reason." She grinned and wiggled her eyebrows. "Want to go lean against the door with me again?"

"No!" Casey stepped into her panties. "Come on, hurry up."

Mica slipped the panties over her hair. The long band, designed to cover the butt crack, extended across her forehead and down her nose. "Do you like my Viking helmet?"

"Impossible. You're impossible. She'll be back any second. Please, stop horsing around and put them on the body part they're designed to minimally conceal."

Mica complied. "Happy? I'm what you could loosely refer to as dressed." She tied the paper sash on the robe and slipped into the paper shoes. "I'm a vision in crinkly paper and ready for my physical now, Dr. Casey."

Their banter was interrupted by another knock at the door. This time it was the young women who were going to do the spraying. "Ready?"

They followed the techs down the hall to the spray booths. Casey disappeared around the corner with her technician, and Mica followed hers into the nearest room. The young woman working with Mica introduced herself as Elissa. Mica took the cap Elissa handed her and placed it over her hair. "When I tell you, please hold your breath. You don't want to get any of this stuff in your lungs while I'm spraying. It kind of stinks."

"I'm paying good money to get stinky?"

"The odor will mostly wash away after your first shower. Try to wait at least eight hours, then pat dry. Don't rub if you want your tan to last. All the information is in here..." The technician's instructions floated over Mica, whose mind swirled with the litany of warnings numbly glanced down at the pamphlet in her hand. "...how to deal with the unlikely event that you have an allergic reaction."

"Huh?" *Great. I don't know why I let Casey talk me into this.* "Thank you."

"Ok, let's go." Elissa demonstrated the positions she'd instruct her client to assume as she coated her body. "Take off your gown and jump in there, and we'll get started."

Mica held her breath while Elissa sprayed her face, until finally given permission to breathe. "Doing ok?" Elissa asked.

"It does stink, kind of yeasty, but not as gross as I read on the internet. The reviews said it would smell like cat pee." As the spray was applied, Mica stretched and bent in all the yoga-like poses Elissa instructed her to do.

"That does it. Now, please remain in front of the fan until you're completely dry. Once you're finished with that, go ahead and get dressed. You might want to sleep on a towel tonight, to prevent staining your sheets. After your shower in the morning, you should be okay. It shouldn't rub off. Enjoy your tan."

Mica thanked Elissa and returned to the dressing room, where she carefully put on her sweats. She heard Casey's voice seconds after the door opened a crack.

"Please promise me you won't laugh."

"Laugh. Why would I laugh?"

"I look like a rusty tangerine." There was an edge of anger to her voice that warned Mica to measure her response. Casey threw the door open and stepped into the changing room.

Mica's hand flew to her mouth. She swallowed hard and bit her cheek. Fearing for her life, she just managed to stop the laugh that yearned to burst from deep inside her. "What happened?"

"She, who shall remain nameless, tells me it'll be perfect once I shower. If that's not the truth, will you bail me out if I come back and do her bodily harm?"

"I promise." Mica opened her arms and Casey fell against her.

"Whatever you do, don't cry. Moisture is our enemy...dryness is our friend. If you leak, your tears might make stripes on your face."

Straightening up, Casey sniffed and stepped back. "You're right. Aaagh. I told you I had a bad feeling."

"About the trip, not about the tanning experience. You're going to be fine. Give it until tomorrow after your shower."

"So much for our having dinner out. I can't go anywhere like this. I look like the bronzed cousin of the Great Pumpkin. I think there used to be a crayon this color."

"Umm. I think they retired it, though." Mica chuckled. "Just saying."

If Mica were milk, no doubt she would have curdled where she stood from the look Casey shot in her direction. "Come on. Get dressed and I'll buy you dinner from the drive through."

"Okay. Do you itch?" Casey began to scratch herself with both hands.

***

While they drove toward home, Casey's color continued to darken into a strange, somewhat blotchy shade of burnished umber. Her skin was hot to the touch, and she was covered head to toe in small, red bumps. "I need you to stop at the drugstore before you take me home. I desperately need a bottle brush. I want to scrub off my skin."

Mica had already called the tanning place, and they did make a run to the pharmacy for the suggested exfoliating scrub. They also got the rubber gloves Mica needed to protect her own tan. They purchased both the tablet and liquid allergy medications, and a soothing gel the druggist recommended to calm the rash. Mica squeezed Casey's hand. "Come on, let's hurry and get you into the shower."

Mica unlocked Casey's front door. The self-described itchiest woman in the world ran past her, shedding her clothing as she dashed up the stairs and headed for the shower.

Naked and no longer modest, she leaned over the bannister. "I need that scrub. Hurry."

They managed to get Casey scrubbed down without getting Mica wet thanks to the extra- long gloves she'd bought, and the dollar-store rain poncho Casey kept in her purse for emergencies. Mica almost laughed, as she ran the sponge doused with the exfoliating scrub over the soaking wet, orange woman.

"Oooh, yessss. There. No, more to the left. Ahhh, umm. Lower."

"It's a good thing that nobody is overhearing you. They'd think I was doing pleasurable things to specific parts of your body."

"Those parts of my body are the only parts not in need of attention at this particular moment."

Mica stepped back. "Okay, shower off. They said to use water as hot as you can stand. You might want to use the scrub again." She stripped off the poncho, as she retreated into the bedroom.

Ten minutes later, Casey stepped from the shower. Mica was waiting with a towel and gloved hands. "Are you feeling any better?"

"A bit. Okay, step back. I don't want to get any water on you. Look at you. You're golden and glowing. Don't take this personally...I hate you."

Mica chuckled and gently patted dry the suffering woman before her. "The rash seems less angry." She stripped off her gloves and plucked the fleecy robe from the hook on the back of the door. She held the robe while Casey slipped into it, then tied the belt and wrapped her arms around the delightfully warm body snuggled against her.

"This isn't anything like I imagined it would be when you saw me naked. I had hopes you'd be focused more on the parts of me that don't itch, rather than all the parts that do."

"I know you got the worst end of this experience. I can't deny I've enjoyed it a lot more than you have. I found several spots I'd like to revisit as soon as you're able to enjoy it." Mica bent her head and sought Casey's lips with her own.

"I'm sorry. That medication has started to kick in. The druggist warned it would make me sleepy, and I'm getting so tired. If I don't lie down, I might fall asleep right here on my feet."

"Let me put some of this gel on you before you drift into dreamland."

"That would be nice. I need to brush my teeth first." Casey reached around and scratched her right butt cheek. "Ugh. I'm miserable. I've never itched so much in my life. Imagine five hundred mosquito bites. At least the shower helped a bit. I'll meet you in the bedroom."

"Those are words I never thought I'd hear from your lips." Mica, tube of gel in hand, retreated to the bedroom. She turned off all the lights except the small nightlight next to the bed and peeled back the covers.

"Yeah, well, don't get your hopes up. Other than you giving me a good scratch, and an application of that gel, I think that's all I'm good for tonight."

Casey finished up in the bathroom and clicked off the light. Modesty long ago abandoned, she tossed her robe onto the bedroom chair. She lay face down, naked on the bed in the dim light. Her body was bright pink from the long and extremely hot shower and the splotchy, bumpy, red rash covering what remained of the blotchy orange spray tan.

Mica sat on the edge of the bed next to her. Using her finger tips, she began to gently soothe the itchy rash. She paused long enough to make a quick observation. "There you go again with those moans and groans. If anyone was listening, they'd expect to hear the sound of you screaming God's name any second."

Casey rolled up on her elbow. "If you know what's good for you, you won't stop, or you'll be screaming God's name begging him to save you."

Mica chuckled. "Okay. Patience. Lie back down. I'll put some of this gel on you."

"That feels nice. It's cooling."

"Roll over and I'll do the other side."

"Just the gel on this side. I'm getting sleepy."

Mica tried to keep her mind on her task. She started with Casey's face, then did her arms and shoulders. All the while, two breasts were waving and calling her name. Her libido was playing the drum solo from *Wipeout* on her heart. No, it was probably closer to Iron Butterfly's *In A Gadda Da Vida*. She stopped and stared. Her palms itched to feel those nipples pebble to her touch. It was her turn to blush, when she realized Casey was watching her struggle.

"Try to think like a doctor." Casey gave her a lopsided grin and winked.

"I'd rather think like a lover." She leaned down and gently placed a quick kiss on the closest nipple, eliciting a quick intake of breath from her patient. "There, now we can both struggle to imagine me as a doctor."

Mica refocused and quickly finished up her task. "Better?"

"Umm. Better really is a relative term, isn't it? Thank you."

Mica returned to the bedroom after washing her hands. She pulled up the covers and gave Casey a quick kiss. "Call me if you need me, or if you're not doing better tomorrow. We can decide what to do. The druggist said you should be showing improvement in a few hours. If I don't hear from you, I'll pick you up tomorrow morning at four thirty. That gives us some extra time for the weather."

"Call me when you get up. I only have a few things to pack, and I'll be ready to go." Casey was snoring lightly by the time Mica pulled the bedroom door closed.

***

At four am, Mica's car heater was blasting out cold air, while she scraped the snow and ice from her windshield. She'd called Casey nearly an hour ago and learned that the meds were helping with the itch. However, the antihistamine made her feel like a zombie.

It took Mica ten minutes longer than usual to make her way to Casey's place. The front door was unlocked, and her bags were waiting at the foot of the stairs. Mica yelled. "You ready to go? The weather is horrible. We need to get going."

"I'm up here. Come on up."

119

Mica was surprised to see Casey standing next to the bed in her underwear. She started to scold her for not being dressed then froze. Her hand flew to her mouth. She pressed her lips together and resisted as long as she could. Tears flowed from the corners of her eyes, as she doubled over in laughter.

Casey stood, hand on hip, waiting for Mica to finish her hysterical outburst. Yesterday's spray tan still clung to her skin in rusty, orange-colored splotches. A rash of angry, red spots covered her from forehead to feet. Peeking between the patchwork of red-dotted, orange patches were a few islands of pale, pre-spray tan skin that she and Mica had managed to scrub clean the night before.

"Got it out of your system yet?"

"Oh God, Casey, I'm sorry I laughed. I couldn't help myself. You look like someone sprayed red paint on orange prison pajamas. Orange is definitely not the new black on you, honey."

Casey joined Mica in laughter, and then quickly burst into tears. She ran a hand over her eyes. "How can I show my face on an airplane? This means I can't go with you."

"I won't go without you. Do you want me to cancel?"

"No! I know you have your heart set on this vacation, and I really want to go too."

Mica stepped forward and wrapped her arms around the woman she couldn't wait to make her lover. "Shh. Come on now, don't cry. She pulled a clean tissue from her pocket and dabbed away the tears from Casey's cheeks. "Nobody will see anything but your face. Let's go see what we can do about that."

Casey burst into fresh tears.

"Oh, sweetie. I didn't mean it like that. You know I think you're beautiful. Well, maybe you don't. I've never had the occasion to tell you what I think." She pulled Casey closer as she cried into her shoulder.

Between sobs, Casey's muffled voice said, "You think I'm beautiful?"

That's got to be one of those 'Does this dress make me look fat?' questions. "Look, honey, I don't want to say the wrong thing here. I do think you usually look beautiful."

Casey sniffed and raised her eyes to meet Mica's. "I didn't know that."

"Unfortunately, today, your beauty is camouflaged by some streaky, rusty colors and a blotchy, red rash."

Casey's eyes filled, but she didn't burst into tears. "How bad is it? If

I wear a turtleneck and a baseball cap, maybe I can cover the worst of the rash with foundation and blush."

"Good idea." Mica glanced over at the clock mentally calculating if they'd make it in time to get to the airport before their flight left. "We need to hustle though. I'll load the car, you get dressed and..." She gestured, waving a hand in a circle in front of her face. "Well...see what you can do. I put my things in your carry-on by the door. I left it open in case you have any last-minute odds and ends you want to put in there."

"Great. I'll be quick."

"I'll load the car, while you get dressed. Just grab the carry-on. Hurry, though. We'll need all the time we can manage to get to the airport. The roads are horrible."

CHAPTER TWENTY-THREE

MICA DIDN'T PAY ATTENTION to Casey, who tossed the carry-on into the back and settled into the passenger seat. Although Mica knew the route to the airport, she was busy poking at the navigation screen, entering in their destination.

"We do know where we're going, don't we?" Casey clicked her seat belt together.

"We do. Maybe there are some detours or traffic warnings though, because of the weather." It wasn't until she clicked her belt into place that Mica glanced up. "Holy shit, Casey! You look like the evil offspring of the Unabomber and the Invisible Man...uh, I mean, woman."

Beneath her hoodie and under her baseball cap, Casey had wrapped her whole head in gauze. "I know. I had to cover my skin, though. I look like the victim of some evil experiment. No sane person would sit next to me on the plane for fear of catching my disease. This way, they'll just think I'm a burn victim."

"Well, I guess it'll work, as long as they don't think you're planning to rob the place."

"I had to do something. While I was awake last night, I checked on the internet and found that cornstarch is soothing for this sort of thing. I put it all over me, including my face. I feel better but couldn't get on a plane looking like a tie-dyed, crunchy cheese snack who fell head first into a vat of flour."

"From now on, we won't have to ever wonder what we'll wear for a Halloween costume. As much as I hate to admit it, you've come up with a clever solution. The bandaged hands were a nice touch."

"Hadn't we better get going?"

"Yes. The roads are getting worse, I'm sure." Mica engaged the transmission and they were underway.

***

The roads were terrible and increasingly slick. They were already late, as they slithered their way into the airport. Casey had taken another dose of the allergy medication. *Oh no, she's sleeping like the dead.* Mica had to shake her to rouse her. "Wake up, honey. We're almost there. I registered us online last night, so we're set except for going through the checkpoint. Here's your boarding pass." She plucked Casey's paperwork from the visor and handed it to her. "I'm going to be running late. Can you check both bags as yours? Mine's not that heavy."

"Sure."

"I'll let you and the bags off up ahead, and then take the car over to long-term parking. We're really late, so go on through and I'll meet you on the plane."

"Okay. Crap. My phone is dead. I didn't charge it last night. I wanted to call Grams and tell her we got here okay."

They both jumped from the car and unloaded the bags. Casey started for the back seat. "Don't worry about that one. It'll be easier for me to deal with that. Just check the two suitcases through, and you won't have to bother with getting anything through screening but you. I'll get the carry-on." Mica fished her own phone out of her jacket pocket. "Here, take mine." She folded her wallet style case back, typed in her access code, and handed her unlocked device to Casey.

Mica slammed the trunk lid and hurried to get back in the car, as Casey called to her. "You have your paperwork and ID?"

"Yup." Mica tapped her pocket to be sure. "I have it. I've got to get a move on. See you in a few." Mica gave a quick wave before she jumped into the car. A blast of arctic air hit her, as she lowered the window so she could see to pull into the airport traffic. Her wipers were iced over and did nothing but grate across the windshield with little effect on the accumulating snow. She squinted through the barely two-inch stripe they'd cleared and searched for the long-term parking lot sign. Two minutes later, the line of crawling traffic dumped her onto the airport loop that allowed people like her, who had missed their destination, to circle back and try again. Unfortunately, there were many others in similar straits in the long line of cars. At last, there appeared a spot to pull onto the shoulder of the road where she could get out of the car and bang off her wiper blades. At least she could now see well enough to find the long-term parking lot.

Mica got her ticket from the machine and started at a jog toward the departure lounge. *Aaah shit! I forgot the blasted carry-on.* Reversing her path, she returned to the car, grabbed the offending bag, and retraced her route. She was already sweating from nerves and hurrying to the terminal entrance, as the warmth of the airport hit her. She fell into step with the other travelers. Casey was nowhere to be seen. Hopefully her trip through screening had been an easy one and she was waiting for her at the gate or on the plane.

Screening seemed like forever, as the line inched forward. Watching the progress of the folks ahead of her was akin to watching paint dry. Still warm, she wiped the dampness from her brow with her sleeve. Finally, it was her turn. Mica emptied the contents of her pockets into the supplied basket and placed her carry-on onto the conveyer belt. The line next to her was staffed by a sweet-looking grandmotherly type, and the one beyond her had the closest thing to a gum-cracking teenager she'd seen since she met Nell. A doughy-looking man about a foot shorter than Mica made eye contact with her and then pulled her bag from the conveyer belt.

"Please gather up your belongings and step over to the table."

"Is something wrong?"

"Random check. Just follow instructions and there won't be much of a delay."

Mica immediately sought her watch in the basket. *Oh man...why me? I hope I don't miss our flight.*

"Good day, ma'am." The voice belonged to a towering hulk of a man. His blond hair was shaved in a crisp crew cut, and his shirt could have stood independently, it was so stiffly starched. The crease in his pants looked razor sharp. *I bet you could slice bread with that. Why didn't I get one of those sweet grandmotherly types?* He approached the table where he emptied her carry-on.

"Is this your bag?"

"Her hesitation caused him to fix her with a piercing, icy-blue eyed gaze. Because, technically, it was a combination of items from both her and Casey, she stammered. "Well, more or less."

"More, or less? Which is it?"

"Yes, it's mine. I'm sharing it with my par..." Mica swallowed. He didn't look like someone who would approve of anyone having a partner, let alone one of the same sex. "Uh...with my business partner."

As he opened her bag and peered inside, his eyes widened. "Has this bag been in your possession since you left home?"

"Well, since I left my partner's home. Yes. I added my belongings to the bag this morning, after she'd put in her things."

"Nobody other than the two of you has had access to it since you left home, or your partner's home?"

Mica nodded. "Yes, that's correct."

"Please get your belongings and step inside this room here." He gestured to a more secluded, curtained room.

"Where are you going?"

"Vacation."

The man, who could have stepped directly from *NCIS* central casting, fixed his steely gaze on her once again. "Where?"

"Uh, Key West."

Again, he gingerly pulled the bag open and peered inside. "What's in the orange sack?"

Casey had to think. "Um, a tent, some bug spray, a lighter...stuff like that."

"Aren't you staying in a guest house or hotel? Why are all these camping items in here?"

Despite Mica being unsure that she even understood why Casey wanted all that stuff, she did her best to explain about their trip to Key West and the week on the rustic island off the coast. He asked her what seemed like an endless list of questions before moving on to the clear plastic box he removed from the bag and carefully set aside.

"Did you put that in the bag?"

"Uh, no."

"Where did it come from?"

Mica shrugged. "I'd guess Casey, my partner, put it in there."

"And do you know what it is?"

"I'm not a hundred percent certain. If I had to guess, I'd suspect it's cornstarch."

"Is your partner a chef?"

"A chef?" Mica bit her cheek to stifle a laugh. "No." Mica shook her head and resigned herself to missing her flight that was about to depart any minute. "Okay, here's the long, sad story. You see, we didn't want to burn with all that sun, so we booked to get a spray tan..." Mica told the steely-eyed, middle-aged, Adonis the story from beginning to end. "She looked like Cheetos left in the fryer too long. This morning, she discovered that corn starch calmed her itching. Which is why I suspect the powder in that container is cornstarch." She thought the man in charge of her fate was going to crack a grin, as she described the invisible woman getup Casey wore to the airport to disguise her blotchy, orange skin.

"Hmm. I do recall seeing her come through. I thought she was a burn victim. What you've told me makes sense now. Your story is so wacky, it can hardly be anything other than the truth. Unfortunately, I still have to test this substance."

Tears threatened to spill over. She blinked them back and garnered enough courage to complain. "I'm going to miss my flight. It's not fair. We would have been here two hours early if not for the weather. Then we had to deal with the tan issue. And now this."

The inspector's steely visage softened for a nearly imperceptible moment. "If you'll give me the details of your flight, I'll call and see what I can arrange for you. He checked his watch. This won't take that long. However, it's safe to assume your flight has taken off." He threw all her items back in the bag and told her to follow him. They moved to another area away from the hustle and bustle. "Sit there. I'll be back as soon as I can."

"Thank you."

The sound of the agent's deep and now recognizable voice drew Mica's attention. "Okay, Ms. Baxter. You're free to go. Our device was able to identify the substance in the container as cornstarch. See the nice people at the ticketing area. I was able to get you booked on the next available flight."

Mica brightened.

"Sadly, all flights are grounded because of the weather. The plane we kept you from catching was one of the last to depart." She glanced at the carry-on. A pair of her underwear protruded out of the middle and prevented the zipper from closing more than half way. "I'm sorry. I couldn't get everything to fit as well as you did. Most of your items are still in there. I removed the lighter...that's a no-no. I hope you'll enjoy your vacation."

Careful not to lose anything from the gaping case, Mica scooped up her belongings and trudged back to the table where other travelers were repacking their bags. It took her two tries to get everything to fit well enough that the bag could zip all the way. Trudging toward the ticketing area, she reached into her pocket for her phone, only to remember that Casey had it, and her wallet case. Not only did her partner have her phone, she had her credit cards and most of her money. She dropped her bag on one of the few empty chairs and stuffed her hand into her jeans. She pulled out fifteen dollars and eighty-three cents. *At least I'm not destitute. Unfortunately, I can't even get in touch with Casey.*

After waiting her turn in line, Mica was pleased to learn that the ticketing agent had good news. True to his word, the TSA inspector had managed to secure her a ticket on the next flight out to Key West. The bad news was that all flights were grounded until the weather broke and they were able to clear the runways of the still accumulating ice and snow.

Mica surveyed the nearly full waiting area. It would be a madhouse before too long. She spied a seat in the corner against the wall and made her way over to it. The person adjacent sat sprawled with long legs extended and wore wool felt fedora, pulled low. Mica tried not to disturb her fellow traveler as she sat down. After stowing her bag under the seat, she plopped down next to her fellow passenger and heaved a sigh. Glancing over at her neighbor, she was surprised to find the traveler to be a woman.

"Not fun is it?"

"Not at all. I'm annoyed I missed my flight. I'm told it was the last one out of here before they canceled everything," Mica slipped out of her jacket.

The traveler sat up and pushed back her hat. "I was on that flight. It was overbooked, and I got bumped. At least they paid me for my troubles." The crow's feet at the corner of her eyes deepened, as she revealed even, white teeth. "I'm Bright. Real name, don't ask." Blue eyes flashed, and the most even teeth Mica had ever seen made another appearance. Bright pulled her hat off, revealing very short, silvery hair. "Ah, what the hell...go ahead and ask."

Mica tilted her head and studied her new acquaintance. More handsome than beautiful, the close-cropped hair seemed to match perfectly her pleasant features and sweet smile. She was one of those people whose looks and demeanor made her feel immediately comfortable to be with. "Okay, I will, first name or last?"

"First. My mother had a weird sense of humor." She turned toward Mica and met her eyes. "You see, my last name is White. It's okay to laugh."

Mica chuckled. "Your mother must be something."

Bright's eyes softened. "Yes, she was."

Extending her hand, Mica said, "I'm Michaela Baxter. Mica to my friends." The woman's hand was warm and smooth, and she held on a tick longer than customary as she studied Mica's face.

"Well, it's a pleasure to meet you, Michaela Baxter. I hope I'll be calling you Mica before the end of this storm."

"Please don't think I'm being sarcastic. If you let me use your phone, you can call me anything you like." She ran her fingers through her hair. "Let me tell you what happened."

Several minutes later, Bright unlocked and handed over her mobile. "Call whoever you want. I'm sorry you've had a tough couple of days."

The tape at the office indicated that Eden and the crew had decided to close because of the weather. Now who to call? Eden's number was on her cell, but she couldn't remember it. She didn't want to worry Grams. Being accustomed to using the autodial in her contacts list, Mica tried to remember Lisa's phone number. It took three tries before she succeeded, and Lisa picked up. "Hi. It's me, Mica. I need your help..."

CHAPTER TWENTY-FOUR

CASEY MADE IT TO the gate just as the rows that included her seat were being called. She dallied until the end of the group started to disappear, before she approached the woman responsible to check boarding passes and herd the people into the passenger boarding bridge. "My traveling companion and I are supposed to be sitting together. She's coming right behind me."

"Okay. We'll keep an eye out for her." She made a quick check of the boarding pass. "I'm sure she'll show up before too long. Move along and the person ahead will direct you. We can seat your friend at the end." The next group started to join the line. Casey didn't know what to do. Would it be better to get out of line and wait, or should she do as she was told? The airline official put a reassuring hand on Casey's shoulder. "Go on now. We'll watch for her."

Casey stifled a yawn, as she walked through the tunnel into the plane. She found her seat next to the window and buckled in. After locating the antihistamine, she unscrewed the cap and took a swig to help with the incessant itch. She prayed it was the proper dose and that she'd be able to stay awake until Mica joined her. From her pocket, she pulled her blow-up neck pillow and breathed fullness into the soft plastic before she placed it behind her neck. Finally, she leaned back, pulled her baseball cap lower, and closed her eyes. It amazed her that nobody questioned the gauze wrapping on her face. Thinking she was burned, the kind woman at the scanner had hurried her through, even asking if she needed a wheelchair to take her to the gate. Thanks to her scrubbing in the shower last night, plus the combination of anti-itch gels, allergy pills, and the dusting of corn starch, the itching was finally starting to abate. The improvement in her comfort level made Casey long to remove the wrapping from her face. Knowing it would be less than four hours until the plane arrived in Key West, she decided to wait until they were in the air to visit the restroom. Once the wrap was removed, a moment of truth would determine if she could ditch the gauze and get away with an application of liquid makeup. *Where is*

Mica? Her desire to open her eyes and search, to talk to the flight attendant, succumbed to the overwhelming sleepiness brought on by the medication.

Casey's eyes snapped open when the captain's voice announced they would soon be landing in Key West. She immediately turned to her right to see a small, grey-haired woman with skin the color of sunburned leather smiling back at her.

"Hello, did you have a good rest?"

Casey put her hand to her head. *Oh my God!* Frantically, Casey searched the surrounding rows for Mica. She closed her eyes and tried to think. *What happened to her?* She patted her pockets until she found Mica's phone.

Her seatmate stayed her with a hand the sun had long ago baked all the moisture from. "I don't think you can use it yet. You'll have to wait until we land."

"Land? Oh, sorry. Thank you. I...uh...sorry." She looked out the window and saw the land below getting closer. *Mica is going to be so pissed at me.* Tears welled in her eyes. *I'll make it up to her somehow.* She looked down at her hand holding Mica's phone. Nestled within the wallet case were Mica's credit cards and several hundred dollars.

Each minute of their descent seemed like an eon in time. She'd never made it to the plane's restroom, so the fact that she was still wearing her gauze mask and baseball cap made her feel claustrophobic. Even the gorgeous view out the window didn't relieve her anxiety. Curbing her initial instinct to climb over the deplaning passengers, Casey chewed her lip until she made it out of the plane and down the stairs to the tarmac. She skirted ahead of the slower passengers and darted through a green door into the building. Already sweating, her first task was to find the ladies room. She set her hat aside. The gauze nearly whistled as she whisked it away. She splashed water on her face to rinse away the cornstarch and scrubbed at her face with the paper towel she plucked from the dispenser. The rash was nearly gone, although there was little that could be done with the splotchy skin. A generous application of blush brought minimal success. She sighed, shrugged, and pulled her cap as low as possible over her forehead. Using another paper towel, she wiped the excess water from the sink and disposed of the gauze before heading for the lounge. While she'd been removing her bandages, she came to a disappointing realization. In her left pocket sat her own cellphone, battery so depleted it wouldn't even turn on. In her right pocket, Mica's was charged but locked. Casey didn't know the code, leaving her with two useless phones.

Exiting the restroom, Casey surveyed the passengers from her flight who were still standing in line waiting for their luggage. She recognized her seatmate and thought she'd take a chance to ask for a favor. The woman looked puzzled and a little wary when Casey approached. "I don't know if you'll recognize me. I sat next to you on the flight."

The woman's eyes opened wide and her head moved backward. The expression on the passenger's face duplicated someone experiencing a train wreck.

"Oh yes. You were the one wrapped like King Tut. I remember. That's one heck of a sunburn you have there."

"Uh...yeah...well, look. I need a favor. I'm sorry. Where are my manners? My name is Casey Harrison."

"Cindy Murphy. My friends call me C.J. Nice to meet you."

"I got separated from my traveling companion, and I need to call home." C.J. asked a barrage of questions. Casey pulled both phones from her pockets as proof of her story. "Look, I have two phones, neither of which I can use. She raised the phone in her left hand. "This one is dead." She raised her other hand. "And this one I can't get into. Do you have one I can use? I'll gladly pay you."

"Sure. You pay for the cab, I'll let you use my phone."

"Deal."

Now that she had phone access, Casey wasn't sure who to call. She tried the office first and got the recorded message that they were closed for the day. After some debate, she decided to call Grams. The call was similar to the famous "Who's on first?" routine, until she finally came clean and confessed that Mica and she were not together in Florida. At least Grams had phone numbers for everyone Casey needed to contact.

At last, she reached Eden, who told her that Mica was stuck in the airport with all flights canceled. "She gave me this phone number you can use to contact her."

"Okay, got it. Anything else?"

"Um, yeah. She said to tell you 7175. She said you'd know what to do with it. This makes no sense to me. Hopefully it'll make sense to you."

"Yes, yes it does." Casey fist pumped. Mrs. Murphy seemed sure the woman she shared her cab with was a walk away from an institution for the certifiable.

"Thanks, Eden."

"Sure. Oh, don't expect Simon to be here when you get home."

Flashes of her beloved tuxedo cat having escaped and come to a violent end flashed before her eyes. "What happened.?"

Realizing Casey wasn't up for teasing, Eden apologized. "Don't worry, he's fine. So fine, I want to kidnap him and take him home with me forever. What a love."

"Phew! You scared me to death. I don't think my frayed nerves can take much more."

Minutes later, the cab dropped Mrs. Murphy at her hotel. Casey returned the woman's phone and thanked her profusely for about the tenth time. Casey couldn't wait to get to her room, so she could call Mica.

***

Sitting with Bright in the airport lounge, Mica finished her tale. She'd always marveled at the idea of telling complete strangers your deepest secrets. People at the gym amazed her with how much information they felt free to share. Two people could meet while working out, and before you knew it, they'd be telling each other their marriage woes, or how ungrateful the children were. Inwardly she chuckled. She was doing the exact same thing with Bright, as she revealed the background of her friendship and budding relationship with her business partner, Casey. In return, she learned that Bright was happily married to her wife. They'd been in a relationship for thirty-three years and had gotten married as soon as it became an option.

"I can't imagine my life without her. We're the original odd couple. She's short and I'm tall, blonde versus dark...well, I used to be dark. She's a detail person, and I'm a conceptualist—an idea person. It's worked for us though. She's a kindhearted woman with a great sense of humor. She has to be, to put up with the likes of me." Bright talked a bit more about Key West, where she and her wife owned a bar and restaurant. After their stories were told, they grew quiet.

"I'm going to head over and check on things. Want anything?" Mica asked.

"I could use some water. Want money?"

"No, water I can afford." Mica meandered off in search of a snack and a couple bottles of water.

***

Fifteen minutes later, Bright answered her phone on the second ring. "Hello. Bright White here."

"Uh. Hello. I didn't catch that. Could you say it again?"

Bright chuckled. "My name is Bright White. Who is this?"

"I'm not sure I have the right number. My name is Casey, and I'm trying to reach my frie...uh part...I mean, my business partner, Mica Baxter."

"Oh, right. Yeah, she's not here right now. She went to see if she can get any information about how long this storm will last. My name is Bright. We're hanging out here in the airport, kind of watching out for each other."

"Is she okay?" Casey's worry forced her to ask the next question. "Is she pissed?"

"Pissed?"

"Yeah, pissed at me for leaving her there? I didn't mean it. I fell asleep. Oh, please tell me she's..."

"Cool your jets, Casey. Everything's going to be okay. You've got a keeper there. She and I will be flying into Key West as soon as things open up here."

Casey didn't know whether it was time for her to exhale a sigh of relief, or to hold her breath over a new worry...the woman had a sexy phone voice.

Bright held the phone away from her ear, as she yelled for Mica to hurry up. The muffled voice became clear again. "Okay, Casey, here comes your honey. It was great talking with you. I look forward to meeting you soon."

At last, Mica's voice came across the airwaves. "Hi, honey. Are you okay?"

"Oh, Mica. I'm so sorry. I fell asleep and..."

"It's okay. Everything will be fine. This is only a little bump in the road. Come on. Tell me how you're feeling."

"I'm some better. For the most part, the itching has stopped." Casey exhaled a long breath. "Wow! I feel like I've been holding that since I woke up on the plane without you. I miss you. Are you okay there?"

"Yes, Bright and I are hanging together. We're doing okay."

"Did I hear it right? Her name is Bright White? Seriously?"

"Yes, that's right. Look, I'd better save the battery on Bright's phone, just in case of an emergency." She laughed at the irony of her own statement. "Well, you know what I mean. I'll call you when we're about to leave here. It may be a while. The storm is stuck off the coast and they recently upped the accumulation totals." She glanced over at Bright who was clearly listening to her end of the conversation. "I miss you, too." Her shoulders dropped as she pushed *End* and handed the phone back to her new friend. "Thanks."

"Come on, cheer up. This, too, shall pass. Remember that absence makes the heart grow fonder."

"You don't understand." Mica hesitated, a little reluctant to reveal intimate details about her fledgling relationship. She hadn't mentioned the little tidbit that today was supposed to be her first time waking up in the arms of her business partner, longtime friend, and new lover...all of whom were the same person. Mica didn't care that Casey's skin looked like she was wearing red and orange toned camouflage. The only thing that mattered was that Mica was miserable without her. "This was supposed to be a honeymoon of sorts."

"Oh, I see." Bright tossed Mica a knowing wink. "Well then, I expect to see you much slimmer after your vacation." Bright chuckled at Mica's puzzled expression. "Kissing alone burns about two calories an hour. Combine more vigorous activities with not coming up for air and food and...you should look like a beanpole at the end of your trip."

Mica blushed and shook her head. Bright was a something of an acquired taste. However, she was growing increasingly fond of the cheerful and good-natured woman with each passing hour. "I guess that explains your build?"

"Could be. I do love my wife. She's the most beautiful and sexy woman I've ever met, inside and out. You'll like her, I think. Remember, Maggie and I are business partners, too. You and Casey will have to come by our place." Bright leaned back and tipped her hat down over her face. "I'm going to take a cat nap. You should try to get some sleep, too. As long as it keeps snowing, we're not going anywhere. Once it stops, they still have to plow the runways."

***

Casey took a shower and assessed the damage. *Oh, I really need to do something about this. Thankfully, the rash is pretty much gone.* Wondering who to call, she thought about Pinky, the friendly woman at the front desk. Despite the warm temp, she threw on her sweat pants and a long-sleeved T-shirt and made her way downstairs.

After a brief discussion, the two women at the desk agreed that the best tanning spa was within walking distance. "You should so go there, they slay." Pinky's friend said.

I hope she's speaking figuratively. Casey took the term as a positive, after Pinky added in reverent tones, "Yeah, they even have an aesthetician."

"Thanks. I'll give them a call." Casey headed back to her hotel room to make the call. The spa receptionist couldn't have been more helpful or optimistic that they could fix her right up. They put her on with Fran, who apparently took pity on her. "Come straight over. I'll wait for you at the front desk."

Casey wasn't sure if she should be worried or encouraged when Fran said, "I've forgotten more about spray tanning than most technicians know." Fran agreed to see her right away and gave her directions for the short walk, so she didn't have time to dwell on possibilities.

"Okay, I'm on my way." Casey headed over to meet the self-described "Goddess of the Spray Tan." With her hat pulled down and the long sleeves and long pants on, she didn't attract much attention as she scooted down the street bound for the spa.

The woman at the desk who introduced herself as Fran, could have been the love child of Lea DeLaria and Danny DeVito. It was a fortunate coincidence that the countertop was glass, so the woman didn't disappear after she jumped down from her stool. Casey followed with her eyes, as Fran oozed herself through the opening between the wall and the counter, where she continued the assessment of her new customer. Her voice was rough and thick with a New York accent. "Oh my. You gotta be Casey. Let's get you inside a room and see the rest of the carnage."

Like a pull toy, Casey trailed down the hall behind the little dynamo and entered the room Fran pointed to. The curtain whooshed closed, leaving Fran outside while Casey followed instructions and stripped down to her underwear. "All clear." The words had barely passed her lips when the curtain flipped back with such speed that Casey almost stumbled backward. Casey was convinced she felt a breeze created by Fran as she circled her like a buzzard homing in on a piece of road kill. "I hope whoever did this to you gets life in prison. Look at this mess they made. You have a naturally olive tone to your skin. The color she used was all wrong, and without a doubt an inferior product. That's why you turned so orange. If you were on the run, all you'd have to do is strip everything off and climb up into a tangerine tree. You'd be invisible to the naked eye."

Casey threw a towel down, slumped onto the bench seat, and dropped her head in her hands.

"Hey, honey. Don't give up yet. We can get this orange color off. No problem. Let's get to it."

Fran tested a small patch of skin with a lemony smelling mixture she'd concocted at her table. "Here's a robe. Put that on, and we'll give it a bit to see if you react to that scrub I tried out on that spot there. I don't expect you will. We want to be sure, though. We need to let that sit there for about half an hour. Do you need anything else done? We can probably fit you in for a haircut, a manicure, or," she gestured pointedly at Casey's panty line, "a wax."

Casey lowered her eyes and hung her head. "I've never had that done."

"Come on. I'll do ya for free. Follow me."

Like a sheep to slaughter, Casey meekly found herself again trailing along after Fran.

"Here." Fran thrust an illustrated leaflet into her hands. "Pick a design you like."

Casey's eyes dropped to look at the different waxing styles pictured on the card. She read the names beneath each of the photos: *Clean As A Whistle, The Landing Strip, The Mohawk, Heart Attack, Martini Glass...* Index finger on her choice, she handed the card back to Fran and blushed. "I think I'd like this one, please."

Fran smiled. "This must really be a special occasion. I don't get many requests for that one." Fran laid out her supplies and invited Casey to get on the table. "So, this is your first wax, you say?"

The application of the warm wax felt good, until Fran peeled off the cloth or paper or whatever that was that ripped Casey's pubic hair out by the roots. To her credit, she only swore twice. However, there was no doubt in her mind she'd cracked at least two fillings from gritting her teeth each time Fran said, "Ready?"

Thirty seconds after Casey thought she could stand no more, Fran bestowed a big grin on Casey and held up a mirror. "Take a peek." By now, Fran had become her most intimate friend. She didn't even flinch when Fran fluffed the remaining hair and commented. "Looks good. Do you like it? We can dye it red if you like."

"Uh...no, thank you. Let's call this good."

"I think it's going to be a real conversation starter." Frans eyes twinkled as she put her hand on Casey's hip and pushed." Roll over and let me check that sample area to see if you reacted to the scrub. Looks fine. Let's go see if we can get this coat of orange spray paint off you."

An hour later, Fran proved she really was the Goddess of the Spray Tan, or at least the Goddess of Spray Tan Removal. Casey stood in front of the mirror and nodded her approval. Her skin glowed. The orange blotches were nearly invisible. Fran had finished her off with a soothing rub down with some magic elixir that made her literally glow. Her skin no longer felt irritated. She nearly wanted to hug her.

She dressed and met Fran back at the product counter. They were the last two people in the spa. "Okay, we've basically exfoliated your body, and bleached the crap that hack sprayed all over you." Fran shoved the first bottle into Casey's hand. "Tomorrow morning, you'll scrub down again with this." She handed her the second bottle. "Moisturize with this one again tonight. Buy one of those little applicator things outside so you can get it on your back. Tomorrow morning, you shower and moisturize again. You should be good to go. The more you moisturize, the better your skin will feel. Avoid beach or pool time for a few days and be sure to protect your skin when you do decide to sunbathe."

"I don't know how I can ever thank you enough."

"One more set of instructions for your nether region," Fran handed her another card. "Follow these directions to the letter. Don't cheat."

Casey read the first line on the directions. "What? You've got to be kidding me. Forty-eight hours?"

"Yes. You should allow the area to heal. Follow the four no-nos...no sun or heat—like saunas or hot tubs—no tight-fitting pants. In fact, it's better if you go without panties and wear only loose cotton shorts or a sundress. No hands. Keep yours and anyone else's fingers and whatever else away from that area to avoid germs. The last no-no is sex." She waggled a finger. "None."

Casey closed her eyes and shook her head. "No sex for forty-eight hours? Please tell me you're kidding."

"No. Deadly serious. Some salons advise twelve or twenty-four hours. I advise forty-eight to be safe, especially since this is your first time. You'll know when it's okay. If you're tender, don't play with it. And if you feel irritated, you can use cold compresses and this lotion."

In the matter of fifteen seconds, Casey had gone from the heights of elation to the deepest depths of the mulligrubs. "I so wish you'd mentioned the no sex part, Fran. But I do thank you for the great job you did on my skin." She paid her bill, gave Fran a generous tip, and started back toward her hotel. After all, Fran didn't know she'd been waiting for weeks to jump Mica's bones. What was another day or two after they'd waited this long? *Just about everything. How will I even begin to explain this to Mica?*

***

Mica and the ticket agent at the reservation desk were on a first name basis, since Mica had racked up marathon-equivalent mileage between her seat and the agent's desk, checking on her flight. Although the snow had finally stopped a few hours ago, they were still working to get the runways cleared. "I think I can get you on the first flight out this morning at 8:49. You'll arrive just after lunchtime. Come back in half an hour, and I'll know for sure. Next flight after that is at 12:25 pm. That one gets in around dinnertime."

Mica plodded back to her seat and gave Bright a thumbs up and an update.

"Thanks. Hey! You've been up for over twenty-four hours. At least I slept some. You should try to get some rest."

"Maybe I can nap on the plane." She sent a text to Casey.

Arriving later this afternoon. Arrival time depends on which flight I can catch. I have a ride from the airport. See you sometime before dinner.

CHAPTER TWENTY-FIVE

THE PLANE TOUCHED DOWN nearly an hour late. As they came into the airport, Bright said, "Come meet my Maggie." She rushed to a woman near the exit, who was sitting in an electric scooter. Kneeling, she buried her face in against her wife's chest. The expression on Maggie's face clearly showed how much she'd loved and missed her partner.

Mica waited at a respectful distance for the couple to whisper their greetings. Eventually, Bright stood up and gestured for Mica to approach. The warmth of Maggie's greeting and welcoming smile made her immediately likeable. "I hear you two have had quite a bonding experience. Thanks for having her back."

Mica grabbed both of their bags and followed behind Bright and her wife. Maggie operated her electric scooter with one hand, while Bright held her other and walked alongside. A handsome guy was lounging against their van. He reached into the back and unfolded Maggie's walker before placing it in front of her. "Hi." The muscular guy stuck out a beefy hand. "I'm Jack, Maggie and Bright's neighbor."

Mica introduced herself and waited as Maggie transferred into the van from the scooter. In a low voice, Bright whispered to her wife, "Is everything okay?"

"Don't worry. I didn't wear my leg, because I've been on it a lot while you were gone... I thought I'd give my skin a rest. We'll be on our feet all night."

"Okay, just checking." Bright and Jack made quick work of folding the walker and stowing it in the back with the bags. Bright drove, pointing out some of the sights, as they headed for Mica's hotel. Before they let her out, she promised them she wouldn't leave the island without a visit to their bar.

***

Mica stopped at the hotel's registration desk, showed her ID, and picked up a key to their room. She was so excited, instead of waiting for the elevator, she took the stairs. After one small detour down the wrong hallway, she found the room and let herself in. Casey was on the balcony as Mica swung the door open.

"Oh, you're here at last." Casey jumped up and ran to circle Mica in her arms. She was wearing a loose fitting, cotton sundress. As per instructions from Fran, she wasn't wearing underwear and had already applied cold compresses and moisturizer twice. She had already served half of her forty-eight-hour sentence of abstinence. She hoped Mica would think the result was worth the sacrifice, since she would be suffering right along with her.

Mica took Casey by the arms and backed her up a step. "You look great, glowing, in fact. How did you get that stuff off?"

"It's a long story. I'll tell you all about it later."

Mica slid her hands down Casey's arms and took her hands. "Look, I'm really, really happy to see you. However, I'm sure it's evident that I haven't had a shower in two days. I desperately need to clean up and brush my teeth before I give you a proper greeting."

Casey wrinkled her nose. "Want me to draw you a bath?"

"Nope. I don't want to sit in there and soak in my own dirt. I'll go take a shower and wash at least two states' worth of grime from my body." She gave Casey a quick kiss. "I'll be right back. Don't give away my spot...or my welcome kiss...to anyone else."

Casey watched as Mica gathered her underwear. "When I finish my shower, would you mind if I have a little nap?" Mica held up her thumb and pointer finger about an inch apart. "Just a tiny one? Maybe you'd like to curl up with me?"

"Of course. You must be exhausted."

Mica laughed. "I was exhausted yesterday. I'm not sure there's a word for how I feel today." Mica looked at her watch and grimaced. "Can you wait until eight to eat? If you can, I'll set my watch and take you on an official date. I'd like you to meet Bright and her wife, Maggie."

"Sure. I'll wait for you on the balcony. Call me when you're done. While you're in the shower, I'll call Grams and let her know you arrived in one piece."

Mica called for dinner reservations before she took her shower.

The hair dryer whirred, as Mica finished up her grooming routine. Minutes later, she came out of the bathroom wearing a sleeveless T-shirt and boxers that clung like a second skin in all the right places. She fell onto the bed and called to Casey. "I'm done."

Casey placed her hand over the phone and answered, "Be right there." It took less than fifteen seconds for her to conclude the call. As she stepped in through the sliding screen, she could hear Mica breathing deeply. Gently, she slipped into the bed next to the woman she loved and studied her relaxed features. Her short, shaggy hair cut fit her face perfectly. A sprinkling of lighter colored strands scattered throughout the honey blonde looked more like highlights than grey hair, although silver was beginning to show at her temples. Her full lips parted slightly, as she sank deeper into sleep. Casey bent her elbow and propped her head on her palm, as she allowed her eyes to roam freely over Mica's body. Her breasts stretched the thin fabric of the T-shirt, revealing the outline of her nipples. Casey itched to run a fingertip across a peak and watch it stand to attention. *The shirt's large armholes would allow easy access to those treasures.* Casey closed her eyes. She felt herself get wet as her desire flared. *Oh, Fran why didn't you tell me about the forty-eight hours before I allowed you to rip my hair out by the roots?*

***

A few minutes before Mica's alarm was set to sound off, Casey returned to the bedroom and sat on the edge of the bed. She was ready to go out, having already applied a cold compress to her nether region, as well as the soothing lotion from Fran. Her skin glowed with moisturizer from head to toe. In fact, she was concerned she might need Velcro to keep from slipping out of bed later.

Staring down at Mica, tears welled in Casey's eyes. *I've wasted so much of my life backing away from people, and even denying my feelings for this gorgeous woman. If she'll have me, I'm going to love her with all my heart.* She looked down at her lap and rolled her eyes. *Well, hopefully, she'll be satisfied just knowing how much I love her, for another few hours.*

"Mica. Do you want to wake up, or would you rather sleep?"

Eyes still firmly closed, Mica's arm snaked around Casey's waist. "Do I have another option?"

Casey knew she was going to have to confess, but she was still basking in the warm, fuzzy feelings of admitting to herself the depth of her love for Mica. She decided that maybe she'd wait until later. There was always a hope that her landscaping down south would soon feel less like a wildfire driving everything from its path, and more like the gentle glow of a hearth welcoming a loved one home. "No, there are no options available if you want to make it to dinner."

Mica's brow furrowed. "Hmm, nourishment of my stomach versus nourishment of a more lascivious nature." She rolled to a sitting position and yawned. "Oh my, that was not nearly enough sleep."

Mica stood and stretched. As she raised her arms, a narrow band of her stomach became visible, and Casey reached out to pull her closer. Mica placed one foot on either side of Casey's legs and moaned as soft kisses were trailed across her bare midriff. Casey sighed and placed her cheek against Mica's warm stomach at the exact moment that her stomach growled. They both laughed. "Sorry. I guess that answers the question of what gets nourished first." She stepped back, and Casey stood to wrap her arms around the woman she hoped would be her lover sooner rather than later.

Their lips met in a gentle kiss. As the heat started to ramp up, Casey pulled back. "I thought you were hungry...and didn't you promise Bright you'd stop by?"

"Aaagh. I am and I did." She sighed and yawned again before she took a step backward. "I feel bad we haven't seen anything of the island because of the stupid storm and airport thing. I imagined we'd...well, I imagined so many things differently. I hope I don't fall asleep on you again tonight."

"You should get a good night's rest. I'll be happy just snuggling with you if that's all that happens."

Mica tugged on Casey's hands and pulled her tight. She slid them down Casey's back. "All healed up? I can't imagine how you got all that color off. You said you had a story to tell me. You must be scrubbed raw."

"You don't know the half of it." Casey put her hands on either side of Mica's face and gave her a peck on the lips. "I'll tell you later. Come on, you promised me food."

They took the elevator down to the dining room and ate their meal. Mica patted her stomach, as she finished all her dessert and half of Casey's. "That's better."

"I bet. For a minute there, I thought you were going to eat the flowers." Casey added a wink to her smile. With the help of the map Casey picked up at the front desk, they walked the few blocks through the warm, fresh night air. The breeze blowing through the palms carried the scents of gardenia, ginger, and orchids mixed with the aroma of salt water. As they entered Bright and Maggie's place, they stopped at the doorway to look around. The ambiance couldn't have been more welcoming, despite the décor resembling something Popeye and Captain Jack Sparrow might have concocted with every nautical item they'd collected in their travels. The two and four top tables dotted one corner of the large room that was divided by the glossy wooden bar. Window shutters were propped open to allow in the cool breeze.

On the other side of the room was a small, raised stage. Soft, upbeat island music played through the overhead speakers. They moved forward when they saw Bright waving from next to the impressive array of alcoholic beverages. Glassware hung from racks above them. Using a cane, Maggie walked over to join her wife and slid an arm around her waist as Casey and Mica approached.

"We saved you a seat over here at the end of the bar. We have a little time to chat before we start to get really slammed. The DJ starts in about a half hour. We do karaoke tonight starting at ten."

"What can we get you?" Bright's eyes sparkled with the obvious look of love she felt for her wife. "If you've never had a Rum Runner, I'd recommend you give one of those a try. Maggie's are the absolute best."

"Sounds good to me." Mica reached for Casey's hand.

Casey grinned and nodded. "Make that two."

The time they had to chat sped by, as demands for Bright and Maggie's services caused them to be away more than they were present. They did tell Mica and Casey about some must do activities on Key West. "I doubt we'll have enough time to fit in too much tomorrow. We're set to leave for the island leg of our vacation. We'll be back next week."

Bright gave them a second round of their new favorite cocktail. "Maybe we'll see you before you go."

"Thanks." Casey took a sip of her drink and tipped her head. "Yes, we'll definitely stop in to see you both before we take off. That's a promise."

"We're holding you to it." Maggie gestured to the band. "It's about to get loud in here, and we're going to get a lot busier. Have fun."

The DJ started off the evening with *Happy.* It didn't take long before he introduced his first karaoke volunteer. Mica tipped her head toward the DJ. "Do you want to sing?" Her eyes were already starting to droop.

"No, let's say goodnight and get back to the hotel. You need some sleep."

"You don't mind? I'm sorry our romantic getaway has been a real bust so far."

"We will have a whole week alone with nothing better to do than make love." Casey grabbed Mica's hand. "Come on, let's go. If you play your cards right, you can make it up to me tomorrow."

Hand in hand, they strolled back toward the hotel to prepare for their first night together. Mica stripped off and slid into bed, waiting for Casey to join her. She pulled up the sheet to cover her breasts, leaving her arms exposed.

Casey, dressed in a lightweight sleep shirt, came around and sat on the edge of the bed. She looked down, studying her fingers, and bit her lip.

"What's the matter? Aren't you getting in here with me? You haven't changed your mind about us, have you?"

"What would make you say that? Have you?"

Mica frowned. "No. Not at all." She reached around Casey and took her left hand in her own, encouraging Casey to shift so she could see her face. "It's just that I've felt like maybe you weren't that interested in...well, you know. I mean, we were ready to heat up the sheets at home. And here..." Mica shrugged her naked shoulder. "I know I fell asleep this afternoon. I'm sorry."

Casey's eyes softened. "No, it's not your fault. And, technically, it's not mine either, although I guess I was complicit in making a poor decision. I blame Fran."

Suddenly fully awake, Mica stiffened. "Who's Fran?"

Casey pictured the rough talking and assertive Fran. "Believe me...nobody you need have concern about." Casey hesitated, not sure how to begin. "Okay, I have something to tell you. Um...remember when you asked me how I got the orange off?" She shifted position and slid her palm across Mica's stomach and around her side, feeling her tremble.

The sharp intake of breath was followed by a small nod.

"Well...I hope you are going to see the humor in this." Casey detailed her introduction to Fran. "We had to wait to see if I'd be allergic to the solution...so I agreed...to allow her to, uh..." Casey sighed and closed her eyes.

"Allowed her to what? You didn't sleep with her?"

"What?" Casey stood up. "Good Lord, no! Well, you see, I wanted to show you how I felt about you...so I allowed her to wax me." Casey raised the hem of her short night shirt for a few seconds to expose

Fran's handiwork. "I thought the heart would say I love you."

Mica's mouth dropped open. She looked up at Casey in a slow motion, frame by frame, gamut of emotions. "Can I see it again?"

Casey raised her gown over her head and dropped it on the floor. Mica reached out as if to touch her. "Don't!" She stepped back out of reach.

"What? Why?"

"It's one of Fran's four big no-nos." She listed the first two. "The last two were no touching and no sex."

"I don't think I like this Fran woman. Seriously, for how long?"

"Until it doesn't hurt anymore."

Mica's eyes glinted. "Maybe I could kiss it and make it better?"

Casey burst into laughter. "You big goof. I just told you I love you, and you totally ignored that."

"I love you, too." She grinned. "Words are sort of anticlimactic to your visual declaration, though." Mica slid over in bed and raised the sheet.

"Oooh, you're naked." Casey joined the woman she loved in bed and snuggled against her. They both sighed as their bodies touched.

Casey's palm felt electric as it traveled over the soft skin of Mica's side and up to her breast, finally finding the nipple she'd so longed to caress that afternoon. They both moaned. "You can't touch me south of the border, but the formidable Fran hasn't had her way with you." Casey slid her hand downward and stopped just below Mica's navel.

"I've waited so long to make love with you." Mica clenched her teeth. "Let's wait until we can both play."

"I can't wait." Casey kissed Mica long and hard, as her hand dipped lower. Mica groaned and separated her legs, allowing the access her lover demanded. Casey lowered her head to Mica's nipple and licked it once. She savored the texture of the erect peak by turning her head from side to side, sliding the sensitive tip between her lips. She continued teasing with her tongue. It was obvious from the sounds that they were both taking pleasure from the sensation. Casey's hand inched lower, teasing.

Breathless, Mica raised her hips. "Inside...now. Please."

Feeling Mica's heat and wetness as she tested the opening, Casey slid two fingers into Mica's warmth. Her own excitement soared, as she stroked Mica into a frenzy. Casey clenched her legs together against her own rising passion. She returned to Mica's mouth and murmured against her lips, "I love you." Casey tensed and came, too, as Mica moaned her release.

Mica reached down and pressed her fingers against Casey's hand. As soon as she caught her breath she whispered, "I love you, too." She inhaled a deep breath of air and blew it out. "That was amazing."

Casey struggled to catch her own breath. "Umm. It was. You didn't even have to do anything. I came just from touching you."

Mica moved her hand away, allowing Casey to withdraw her fingers. "I have only one question to ask you...why did we wait so long to do this? God, we've missed so much." Mica adjusted her position and rolled to her side, as Casey rolled back against the pillow.

"I take full responsibility. I admit it. I'm so glad you didn't listen to me."

Mica kissed Casey's forehead and worked her way down to her lips. "Shall we see if we can do it again?"

"I can't..."

"I know. Fear not, I won't travel to the heartland." She chuckled and lowered her tongue to Casey's breast. "We can enjoy my touring the rural areas, though, and see if the heartland can be happy about the non-central areas being visited."

Casey grinned. "I had no idea you had this much interest in geography."

Mica allowed her hand to wander over Casey's breast. "I think I'll start with a thorough exploration of this mountainous area right here."

CHAPTER TWENTY-SIX

A ROOSTER CROWED, AND Casey's eyes fluttered open to meet a set of emerald-green eyes under tousled golden-blonde hair. Her lips curled into a satisfied grin. "Morning."

Mica leaned over and placed a soft kiss on Casey's mouth. "Morning to you, too. You were sleeping with a smile on your face."

"That's because I'm happy. I feel like I've finally got it all. I'm in love with my best friend and she loves me back. We already know we're compatible in most ways. I admit it's a relief to know we're compatible in bed. I've been a bit anxious about it, I'll admit."

"Umm." Mica trailed her hand down Casey's torso, coming to a stop just north of the area she'd promised not to touch last night. "How much longer until I can explore the southern wetlands?"

Casey chuckled. "Probably tonight. I think the management has to do a final inspection and decide if it's ready to open for business as soon as the forty-eight-hour strike ends this afternoon."

"So, let's go kill some time sightseeing until…uh, other opportunities open up."

They both laughed. Casey rolled over and rested her head on Mica's shoulder. "Are you happy?"

"Oh yeah!" Mica squeezed Casey's shoulders with her arm and pulled her tighter. "Absolutely. I feel like I finally have everything I ever wanted." Following a pregnant pause, she added, "Except maybe food. I'm hungry. Breakfast?" She turned her wrist to see the time. "Ooh…maybe brunch."

Casey and Mica took turns in the shower, dressed, and went downstairs to eat. During their meal, they looked over the brochures detailing different points of interest they could see. In consideration of the short time remaining, they agreed to forego swimming and snorkeling until they reached the island. They both wanted to visit Fort Jefferson, Hemingway's home, and Truman's Little White House. To cover as much ground as possible, they decided to rent bicycles and do an overview tour. They pedaled to the southernmost tip of the Key. The traffic was a mixture of cars, motor bikes and cycles, bicycles, and people on foot. Tourists shopped and strolled, while chickens and cats meandered along the street in front of them as they pedaled past shops, bars, and interesting architecture. They stopped in Mallory Square, where street performers entertained groups of tourists. Despite Key West's reputation of being a gay mecca, the crowd was mixed. They noted the huge cruise ship in the harbor and wondered if its passengers accounted for the makeup of the largely heterosexual swarm of people in and near the popular tourist area. After watching the fire eater and juggler, they lingered to watch some other street performers before joining the line waiting to have a photograph taken next to the stubby red, yellow, black, and white buoy marking the southernmost point in the United States.

Between using the map and asking directions, they found their way to Duval Street and worked their way north. They parked their rentals next to a row of other bikes, and felt thankful they hadn't rented a car. Parking was obviously difficult at best.

They strolled up the street, occasionally stopping to window shop or make a foray into a store that interested them. They bought straw hats. Casey chose one with a wide brim, while Mica opted for a more traditional Panama style. A bit further down the road, they stopped for an afternoon drink at an open-air bar and enjoyed listening to the guitarist as he sang and played for the audience. As the afternoon hours faded, the couple reversed direction and pedaled to their hotel, returned the bikes, and had dinner.

Back in their room, Mica opened the wine they'd bought that afternoon and poured them each a glass before joining Casey on the balcony to watch the sun go down and reminisce about their day. "I'll be right back." Mica disappeared inside for a few minutes. Upon her return, she leaned over and kissed Casey. She smelled of toothpaste and soap. Taking Casey's hand, she grinned. "I've enjoyed our little journey around the island today. Now, I do have in mind some exploration of the local underbrush in the heartland. Care to be an active participant?"

Casey stood and wrapped her arms around her lover, although she couldn't help giggling. "Very much so. Go ahead and get in bed, and don't start without me. This is a journey we should take together." They walked inside hand in hand. Minutes later, Casey came out of the bathroom wrapped in a towel and approached the bed.

Mica reached out a long arm, grasped the end of the terry cloth concealing her lover, and tugged.

Naked, Casey snuggled into the warmth of her lover, who wrapped her in her arms and rolled so that Casey settled full length against her. Casey dropped her head into the crook of Mica's neck and inhaled the familiar scent of the woman she loved.

Mica's hands roamed the length of Casey's back, exploring her torso inch by inch, until she could reach no further. She spread her legs, tipped up her hips, and settled Casey against her. "Umm. That's a new sensation. It feels good. I've never been with a woman who's been waxed like that before."

"Aside from the fact that you just shared too much information, here's fair warning. Don't get used to it. It was an unpleasant experience in oh so many ways."

Mica chuckled and rolled again until she was in the top position. Soon they became serious about what they were doing, as Mica began to make love to her. The fire between them built as Mica's tongue tested the different contours and textures of Casey's skin. Mica thoroughly explored her lover's breasts and teased one of the erect nipples with her tongue, as her palm rolled over the other, drawing a moan from Casey's lips and a sharp increase in the rate of her breathing. Mica inhaled the scent of her lover, as her mouth dipped lower.

Casey's hand stopped Mica's journey. "Wait. Please."

Mica raised up and searched Casey's face. "What's the matter? Did I do something wrong?"

"No." Casey closed her eyes for a few seconds, gathering courage. "I've never let anyone do that to me, nor have I ever felt the desire to do it to anyone else.

"It's okay. If you don't want me to, there are lots of other things to do. Tell me what you like."

"I didn't say I didn't want you to do it. See...I always felt it would be something special, something I'd share with the woman I planned to spend my life with. That woman is you. I love you, Mica."

"I love you, too. Let me show you how much." Using her tongue, Mica brought Casey to the peak, only to back off before bringing her there again. At last, only after Casey was begging for release, did Mica deliver on her promise.

CHAPTER TWENTY-SEVEN

THE SOUND OF A rooster's insistent crowing woke them. Mica was spooned against Casey's back. She kissed her neck and trailed her hand down Casey's stomach, moving lower, until she reached the heart-shaped patch of hair she'd paid considerable attention to the night before. Casey shifted her position, as Mica's hand brushed through the soft curls. Mica inched lower and claimed her reward as Casey closed her eyes and smiled. "I love touching you. You're so responsive." Mica moved lower and felt Casey's clit harden. Seconds later, they were moving together, fingers gliding smoothly in and out, until they both came.

"I like waking up with you, Ms. Baxter."

"And I think there's nothing hotter in this world than you, Ms. Heartland."

They both chuckled.

"Hey, look what time it is. We still need to shower, pack, and eat before we go to the dock. The hotel said we could leave one of our bags here, until we return to spend our last day and night in Key West."

***

The sun was shining as they met the agent for the roughly fifteen-minute boat trip to the island. The odor of rum permeated the air around Dan, as he directed them to follow him down to the boat tied at the pier below. Casey arched her brows and opened her eyes wide as if to question the wisdom of their decision. Mica shrugged, hoping the cloud surrounding Dan was left from the night before and not the morning's hair of the dog. His slight Southern drawl wasn't slurred, and he seemed stable enough as he untied the boat and nimbly hopped aboard. They navigated through a harbor filled with boats of many shapes and sizes. A different passenger cruise ship was docked for the day, again increasing the population of Key West with a new group of tourists.

It didn't take long for their destination to come into view. Rising from the clear, blue water was a divot of land, maybe two acres in size, covered by palm trees and scrubby underbrush. A small spit of sand extended along the edge, next to the wobbly looking dock. "Watch your step," Dan instructed, as they made the transition from boat to dock.

"Come on, I'll show you the lay of the land." Like ducklings behind a mother duck, they trailed Dan along a rocky path toward the hut.

Mica glanced at Casey, as she pointed a shaking finger toward a two-foot-long iguana sunning on a rock. "Uh, Dan?"

"Don't bother him, and he won't bother y'all. There are a few of 'em on the island. He's one of the medium-sized guys. There are some interesting bugs here too, an' the sea birds stop by every now and again." A few feet farther, Dan stopped and showed them the generator station. "She's all set to come on by herself. She only runs for a couple of hours, three times a day. You can add gas from those cans over there if she runs out, but you should be good for the week without having to fill up. We only run her to cool down the fridge and pump water into the holding tank for flushing. I delivered a few cases of drinking water earlier and stocked up the pantry and the fridge for y'all. Try to stay out of the fridge 'cept around meal times. That'a way, things'll last longer."

Their accommodations came into view. Mica had hoped the word *hut* was Dan's quaint term of endearment for where they'd be staying. Sadly, a more apt description might have been "semi-solid structure with great ventilation."

"Cooking is there." Dan pointed to a propane grill with a side burner, then a short distance away to a fenced in area. "Cans are over there. Be sure to put the trash in everyday and lock 'em down tight. There's a Jet Ski at the other end of this path. Contract says use at your own risk. Don't worry about that. It works good. We do get some jackasses out here that do stupid stuff once in a while. So, the owner added that clause to the contract to protect himself from lawsuits." Dan tipped his hat, preparing to leave. "Oops, almost forgot. There's a long-range, two-way radio inside, if ya have an emergency or need me to bring anything over.

He led them to the hut and entered through the side door. Three people filled the small space. "There's a nice deck outside. Beautiful sunsets. Best view on the island." He tried to open the sliding glass door and had a hard time. He managed to get a shoulder into the opening and pushed back with all his strength. The door squealed its protest of the abuse and begrudgingly gave up an opening to the outside deck. "I'll bring some silicone spray back for you. I'll leave it on the Jet Ski tomorrow morning, so I don't bother y'all." He pointed around the far side of the hut. "Bath is out there. Any questions?"

Mica and Casey looked at each other. Mica answered for both of them. "I don't think so, thank you."

"Unless I hear from ya, I won't be returning until your time is up. Okay, you're on your own. Have a good time." Dan turned and abruptly hurried down the path toward the boat.

The two women turned toward each other and quickly looked away to stop the laughter they each knew would burst forth if they continued eye contact. As Dan disappeared from their view and earshot, Casey asked. "Why do I feel we were just stranded on a deserted island?"

Mica smirked. "Because we were?"

"Well, there is that..."

"Come on." Mica stuck out her hand. "Let's go see what Dan failed to reveal about the inside of this luxury accommodation."

Casey squeezed Mica's hand and followed along as they went back inside. The side door they'd originally entered through was at the head of the bed. The interior probably measured twenty by twenty feet. The refrigerator, sink, and counter occupied one wall. Opposite the fridge stood a large pantry cabinet. The bed was covered with a colorful comforter and formed a right angle with the sofa. The storm shutters were open above both. The huge triple slider was across from the sofa and flanked by two narrow bookcases. Casey pointed to the four holes in the screen that covered one panel. There was no sign of a screen for the panel Dan had forced open. "Air conditioning?"

Mica raised an eyebrow and nodded at the pantry. "Dare we look to see what's to eat?"

She started for the cabinet on the far wall but drew up short when Casey pointed. "Watch out. Watch your head."

A huge fixture of woven palm fronds hung just above Mica's head. The leaf shaped fan was suspended from the ceiling. A rope ran from a hook on the wall, up over a pulley, then attached to the bottom of the fan. "I think this is the air conditioning." Mica loosened the rope from the hook and pulled to raise and lower the fan, creating a slight breeze. "Wouldn't you work up a sweat tugging on this?" She raised the fan higher against the ceiling. "Must have been short people here before us," she said with a straight face, before she continued to her destination.

Mica opened one door of the pantry. "Hmm. Come here. Look what we have."

Casey approached, wrapped an arm over Mica's back, and pulled open the other door. They were faced with an array of canned meats, soups, rice, various shapes of pasta, and sauces. "Wonder what we're supposed to use the grill for?"

"Fish? Maybe they're thinking we'll fish. Although it's not necessarily a gourmet menu, we won't starve to death." Mica stood up. "There's only one thing missing."

Casey looked around. "What?"

"I suspect after eating all this yummy food, we might need a bathroom."

"Oooh. Where is it?"

They went out through the open side of the slider and stepped onto the wrap around deck. Two deck chairs faced the gorgeous water view. "Hey, here's a plus. Like Dan said, gorgeous view." Mica continued around the side of the hut and found a set of steps. At the bottom, a path led to the "light and airy bath." It was essentially four posts in the ground. Four sheets of plywood painted a deep forest green made an enclosure. Mica tugged on the handle to reveal a clean but rustic bathroom. The laundry tub doubled as the bathroom sink. There was no curtain around the shower head fitted to a hose that dropped from a pipe in the wall. "Good thing it's warm here. I don't think there's going to be a lot of hot water. Looks like they just have a little propane heater out there, so don't plan on long, steamy showers. That appears to be the extent of the heating the brochure mentioned."

Casey wrapped her arms around Mica. "I'm sorry. I thought I was doing a good thing getting you this vacation. You seemed to want it so badly."

"I don't think this is exactly what either of us expected. We had fun on Key West, though, and we have each other. That's what is most important. Although it's not luxurious, it is private. Exploring the water around us should be fun. Come on. Let's go skinny dipping."

They grabbed towels from the cabin and made their way to the dock, where they found masks in a wooden box. At the water's edge, they stripped down, and Mica slathered sunblock on Casey before they slipped into the sea. Once they adjusted to the cool temperature of the water, they used the goggles to explore the ocean floor. They enjoyed watching several different kinds of fish swim below them. They even saw a turtle and an eel as they paddled around the refreshing water.

Casey waited until Mica's head popped up. She wrapped her legs around Mica's waist and shivered. "I'm freezing."

"Come on, I'll warm you up." They spread their towels on the sand and curled up together. The sun warmed them, as they explored each other's bodies with lips and hands, and talked about everything and nothing as lovers do. As the sun started to drop and the air cooled, they wrapped in their towels and made their way back to the house.

"Go ahead and take your shower, Casey, while I make us some pasta for dinner. It seems the least offensive choice."

"Um, great." Casey grinned. "I was trying to figure out how we were going to grill that canned ham." Before she left, she called back over her shoulder. "I'll try to keep my shower short. You still have yours to take, and we'll have the dishes to wash."

They ate on the deck, finishing their meal and enjoying the gorgeous golden view. The sun was turning the sea shades of orange and yellow as it kissed the sea. Casey and Mica held hands as they watched the last of the sun dip into the ocean. There was a sudden drop in the temperature as the wind started to kick up.

"That was gorgeous." Casey squinted at the darkening sky. "Are those rain clouds in the distance?"

"I don't know. I didn't check the weather this morning. We've been on the go all day."

Mica lit the lantern and got them each a sweatshirt. They sat on the deck talking about their trip to the island and laughed about their disappointment at seeing how primitive their lodgings were, until they grew chilled. "Do you want to get into bed, so we can get warm? I think I'll close the shutters on the windows. It's starting to blow pretty good." She'd struggled but finally succeeded in closing the shutters. Mica returned about ten minutes later and slid into bed with Casey. "Mmm. You're nice and warm."

"Slide over here and let's see how hot we can get you." Casey kissed her way down Mica's body. It was Mica's turn to stop her. "You don't *have* to do that."

"I love you, and I've waited all my life to find someone I wanted to share that much intimacy with. I'm so glad it's you."

Exhausted and satisfied, they didn't care that the bed was lumpy; they only cared that they had each other.

CHAPTER TWENTY-EIGHT

THE THUNDER WOKE THEM just past midnight. The wind was blowing the rain in through the sliders. Mica got up and slid one of the doors closed. The second door, the one Dan had forced, wouldn't budge. Casey joined her in trying to close the heavy glass pane. "It must be off the track." The rain blew in like the power spray in a car wash. Casey looked around. "There's nothing for us to put over it?"

Mica shrugged. "There's the quilt on the bed. It's already pretty wet. How would we secure it?"

"All that stuff we brought with us...too bad we didn't bring a hammer and nails. We could use the tent. Can we use the cord from the fan?"

"Maybe we should just get in the tent."

"Out there, on the deck?" Casey shook her head. "No thanks."

"No, in here."

"Oh, great idea." Casey got the carry-on and pulled the smaller bag from inside.

Mica got the lantern, saying a silent thank you that it was battery powered. They unfolded the emergency tube tent. Using the cord included in the packaging, they supported the tent enough that they could slide in and not touch the walls, so they wouldn't break the tension and suck water inside. They unfolded and covered themselves with the emergency blankets they'd brought with them. The tent rippled around them, as the wind blew into the hut. Thunder and lightning crashed and flashed with terrifying frequency.

Casey reached for Mica's hand. "Looks like another sleepless night."

"I'd have bet a million dollars we'd never have used this tent."

"Although I think I read the brochure more carefully than you did, I didn't expect this either." Casey took a deep breath. "Mica? What would you do differently with our business or your life if you could afford to do anything you wanted? You know, like if you won a lot of money."

"I'd have stayed in Key West and forgotten this place."

"Come on, I'm serious."

"Okay...so I have a million dollars." Thunder shook the room. "Wow, that was close." Mica shivered and pulled Casey closer before she returned to the discussion. "As to my life, I wouldn't change a thing. I have you, and I'm happy. I love what we do for a living. I guess maybe I'd build or move our business to a larger facility. I'd get some more equipment for Grams and Millie's group in the corner and expand their area. Maybe I'd put in a little coffee shop where they could sit and chat, play cards, or whatever. I'd also like to do something with kids. You know, get them started early with physical fitness. Maybe we could figure out a way for the little ones and the older folks to do more together. What about you?"

"Well, I've had a lot more time to think about this than you have. I'd help our friends, financially. Like I'd help Eden with tuition money, so she could take the time she needs to finish her research. I'd give Trish a raise, a nice one, because she deserves it. She has an interest in record keeping or accounting. As much as I'd hate to lose her in her current position, I think she'd stick with us if she got her accounting degree. Serena told Lisa she'd like to become certified as an interpreter, or maybe take some cooking classes and have a small place of her own. Things like that." She paused. "Ooh, I almost forgot the best one. I'd send Grams and Millie on a cruise around the world. Hell, maybe I'd send the whole corner group, if any of them wanted to go. For Grams and Millie, I'd hire someone who would help them remain independent. I'd donate to some good charities who actually help people, too.

The wind rustled the tent. "Wow. You cheated. That would cost much more than a million dollars."

"Well, maybe we could do everything we wanted if we had more than that. Like maybe say, uh...just over three million after taxes."

Other than the howling wind, Casey heard nothing but silence.

"That's a very specific amount of money."

"Yes, it is. It's a good thing you're lying down. Remember that lottery ticket you bought on New Year's Eve?"

"Yeaaah." Mica drew out the word. "I bought it, but you paid for it."

"That doesn't matter. If you hadn't gotten it for me, we'd never have won the lottery."

"Nooo.

"Yep. Five million on the scratch-off. It's worth over three million after taxes."

Mica sat up and raised her voice. "And you let us come to this shitty island?"

Casey laughed until tears came from her eyes. "I did. You'll always have this you can point back to and say, 'Before I won the five million, I was sleeping in a tent, inside a hut, with an outdoor toilet.'"

Mica got to her knees and crawled out of the tent.

"Where are you going?"

"To get that walkie-talkie before it gets ruined by this weather. We're getting out of this place as soon as humanly possible."

Casey giggled.

"You're sure we really won that much money?"

"Positive. Now, let's get that gadget out of the weather."

While the storm raged, the walkie-talkie proved useless that night. The following morning dawned crisp and clear, with the air smelling freshly scrubbed. They were awake early and tried the walkie-talkie again. A set of tin cans and a string would probably have been more effective.

Resigned to their fate, they tried to clean up some of the water that had come in during the storm. Casey was hanging the comforter over the deck rail, when she heard someone holler a greeting. Dan showed up to check on them and deliver the silicone spray. "Nobody expected that storm. It was a bad'un. You gals okay?"

"Mica, Dan's here. We're getting out." They didn't ask, nor did Dan offer, to contact the owner to get their money back. Neither of them cared. They were happy enough that the hotel was able to give them a room.

They ate a decent lunch at an alfresco restaurant, where Casey went through what happened to the lottery ticket from the minute Mica purchased it until Casey contacted the lawyers. "I have our lawyer and our accountant working on how best to handle things. There was barely time between when I realized that we'd won and when we had to leave. So, I've got them researching everything while we're gone. I was going to tell you sooner, but then everything went so haywire..."

"In all the time I've known you, that has to be the biggest understatement you've ever made. I still don't understand why you didn't tell me sooner—like when the blizzard hit, before we left for the airport. We could have stayed home and chartered a private plane the next day, or hired a limo to drive us down, or..."

Casey's eyes filled. "I'm sorry, Mica. I wanted to surprise you. I wanted to tell you about it in a romantic way, on our romantic vacation, and..."

"Oh, honey. I'm being ungrateful." Mica took her hand. "Don't you think cuddled up and soaking wet in a tent, in gale force winds, is romantic? I do. Come on, let's go enjoy our vacation."

That afternoon, they took a cruise on the glass-bottomed boat and stopped to say farewell to Bright and Maggie before they went back to the hotel to pack for their early flight home.

The alarm on Mica's watch sounded the next morning. With her eyes still closed she said, "Honey, I had the craziest dream. We were on this island and...well that's not the weirdest part. I dreamed you told me we won five million dollars in the lottery."

Casey pinched her.

"Ouch!"

"You deserved that. You know we won."

They both burst into laughter.

"Come on, get up. I can't wait to get started on our new life together. I hope our trip home is less eventful than our journey here."

.

CHAPTER TWENTY-NINE

SIMON SETTLED ON MICA'S chest and licked her chin. "Aaagh, Simon. I love you, but I'd prefer that you go lick your mother's face."

"He woke me ten minutes ago with his new favorite tactic." Casey laughed and wrapped her arm around her cat and her lover. Simon squirmed free with a meow and gave them a dirty look as he jumped down.

"I'm so glad you're home. I missed you," Mica said.

Casey had returned late the night before from escorting Millie and Grams on a week-long cruise in appreciation of all their hard work. Thanks to them, the new snack bar is whipped into shape and fast becoming Fit As A Fiddle's social center. Mica had stayed behind to finish up some last-minute details related to their business, because she and Casey would be taking a vacation of their own soon.

The delay and late arrival of their plane meant that when Mica picked them up, it was long after their normal bed time when they'd delivered Grams and Millie back to her grandmother's house. Despite Casey and Mica's separation of a week, the exhausted couple had fallen into bed and done nothing more than spoon together in sleep after a few brief kisses.

Eyes opened into mere slits, Casey rolled over and slid a leg across Mica's, as she snuggled against her. "Good morning, sweetheart. Happy anniversary. It's hard to believe we've already been living together for a year."

"I know. Although it took us several months until we made it official and moved in together, from the time we returned from Key West, we were either at your place or mine. Your place was nicer and bigger, so we ended up here." Mica spread her legs, as Casey's roaming hand found its way to her warmth and begin a slow tease. "They say that time flies when you're having fun. We've been doing that, haven't we?"

Casey smiled when Mica pressed up against her fingers, giving encouragement. "Mmm." Mica's breathing increased with Casey's tempo.

"I got a present for you." Casey whispered.

"You...did...hmm...let me guess." Mica sucked air in through her teeth. "Don't stop. That feels so good." Casey loved that Mica moaned as she chased down the path of pleasure, tensing before she fell back spent. She breathed out a contented breath and pulled Casey up for a kiss. They snuggled for a few minutes. "I like waking up with you." She took a minute for her breathing to settle. "So, tell me about this present you got me, or was that just it?"

"No. You're so fresh." Casey laughed. "Remember the surprise I got you when we went to Key West."

Mica rolled over and stared, eyes wide. "Oh, no. You didn't. The heart? I couldn't touch you for forty-eight hours, and you were in misery for a month afterward, until all the hair grew back. You swore you'd never do it again."

"Oh no. I will never, never, never do *that* again. I felt like a naughty Chihuahua. I had a nearly uncontrollable desire to hump every stationary object I saw, just to scratch the itch." The picture Casey painted made them both giggle. No...it's something else, although you're on the right track. Why don't you see if you can find my present?"

Mica pulled the sheet down to Casey's waist and explored with her fingers and her lips. Inch by inch, she exposed more skin until she saw the heart on Casey's stomach just above Casey's pubic hair. "A heart tattoo?"

Casey nodded. "Don't be worried. It's only temporary." She giggled. "I couldn't resist. If you like it, I'll get a real one. We have time to think about it while we're on our trip in Key West. No island, no spray tan. Just a luxury hotel room and us."

"I love it. Let me show you how much." Mica leaned down and kissed the heart present. Before she continued her journey lower on Casey's body, she grinned. "I do like it. Maybe we should get matching ones."

***

The journey to Key West was much less eventful than the first time they went. Bright picked them up at the airport and delivered them to their hotel. Out of Casey's line of vision, Bright winked at Mica. "I made dinner reservations for you, as you asked, Mica. Everything's taken care of." She gave a jaunty wave as their friend pulled away.

"What's that about?"

Mica smiled. "I'm taking you out for dinner tonight, to a special place Bright and Maggie recommended. They made reservations for us. We need to take a ferry there, so we need to be at the dock at five-thirty. We'll have time for a swim, a nap, and maybe a whatever."

"A whatever, eh?" Casey glanced at her watch and tried not to grin. "I think I should always let you plan our vacations. I like your itinerary so far." She kissed Mica's cheek before they picked up their bags and entered the hotel.

Suitcases unpacked, they made their way down to the pool where they spent a lovely couple of hours alternating between sunning and swimming. Mica unlocked the door to their room, went inside, and waited for Casey to step into her embrace. "I love you, Casey."

"I love you, too, sweetheart. Shower?"

"Umm." Mica kissed her lover as they made their way into the shower, shedding clothing as they went. In the shower, they took turns soaping and washing each other, paying special attention to the most sensitive areas. "Darn, I dropped the soap."

Casey chuckled as Mica lowered herself, sliding along the length of Casey's body. As Mica's mouth found her center, Casey managed to gasp out, "I love the way you search."

Later, cuddled in bed, they talked about their last year together. Casey traced her hand over Mica's ribs, coming to rest on her breast. She massaged, more for their shared pleasure than to excite, both feeling happily satiated for the moment, following their shower. "It's hard to process how much has happened, both personally and with the business, since we were last here in Key West a little over eighteen months ago. I can't believe we moved in together a year ago. How quickly time flies."

"I know." Casey kissed Mica's forehead and slipped from the bed. "The final phase of our business plan will tie everything up nicely. We'll have done everything we planned once we open the child care area."

"I know. Is it being too much of a workaholic to say I can't wait to get everything finished and prepare for the grand opening?"

Casey laughed. "Maybe just a little. We did just get here, and everything back home is in good hands." She pulled Mica to her feet. "Come on, we need to get dressed and down to the dock."

The ferry ride to the offshore Key where the restaurant was located was perfect. The temperature was warm and they found the cool breeze blowing across the water refreshing. After their arrival, they had time for cocktails at the bar while their table was being made ready.

Returning to the Keys put them in a reflective mood, and conversation eventually turned to their business achievements. "I'm so happy with the new location for Fit As A Fiddle." Mica propped her chin on her palm, her feelings showing clearly in her eyes as she met Casey's own love softened gaze.

Their new center was in a small strip mall, across the street from an over-fifty-five apartment complex. At first, everyone was shocked to hear that the food store was leaving the shopping area. Joy followed concern when they heard that the store wasn't really closing, only relocating, and they would reopen in a newly constructed building across the street. Casey and Mica renovated the space vacated by the grocery market, and moved their business into the larger, custom designed space. Casey and Mica had realized their goal of expanding the role and function of their state of the art PT facility.

"Yes, we did a much better job with our new business than we did with our first trip here. Remember? Everything that could go wrong, did go wrong on that trip." Casey reached for Mica's hand and smiled in remembrance of their achievements since their last trip to the Keys. "I guess we paid our dues and the gods chose to smile down on us ever since. Although not totally without issue, our renovation was relatively painless, as I look back on it."

"There are always those gut churning delays, though. I thought we'd never finish the renovations." Mica exhaled in memory of the stress they'd been under getting everything done on time and within budget. "They say that it always takes twice as long and costs twice as much as you budget. Luckily, we managed to get through the renovation without too much additional expense. Thankfully, the food store that occupied the space before us, left such an open canvas. Between us, we kept things moving forward. Even though it went well, it was nerve wracking. I still find it hard to believe we got everything done on time."

They were told that their table was ready. Because it was still hot and humid outdoors, they'd opted to sit inside at a romantic corner table with a beautiful, unobstructed, westward looking view. They ordered their appetizers, as the sun began to drop toward the sea. As the meal and the magnificent sunset progressed, they enjoyed making small talk that happy couples do. Mica and Casey finished their shared key lime pie just as the brilliant reds and oranges of the sunset began to fade. "This is what we should have done the last time we were here instead of going to that so called romantic island." Mica used her fingers to make air quotes to emphasize the word romantic. "To be fair, the storm wasn't their fault."

Casey chuckled in recollection. "I thought Lisa and Serena were going to die laughing when we told them about that. We've done well for ourselves, despite a not too auspicious start."

"I think so too. And so have they. I'm happy that they worked through the issues keeping them apart and are now as happy together as we are."

Mica glanced at her watch. Her leg was jiggling under the table.

"Are you going somewhere? That's the fourth or fifth time you've looked at your watch."

"No, although don't want to miss the ferry back. It leaves in twenty minutes. Ready?"

"Sure."

The ferry returned to Key West, where they strolled hand in hand back to their hotel. Mica unlocked the door and flipped on the light, pleased to see that room service had done as she asked.

"What's all this?" Casey pointed at the table containing a beautiful bouquet of roses, a chilling bottle of champagne, and a beautiful tray of fruits and chocolates.

Mica crossed the room, popped the cork on the champagne, and poured some bubbly for each of them. Casey approached and joined Mica in a toast to their happiness. They clinked glasses. "It's a small celebration for us. I love not only you, I love us. I feel that together, we've found the happiness we've each individually sought for many years. Even though I wish we'd found it sooner, I don't think I'd change a thing. There has always been something special between you and me. Tonight, I'd like to make *us* more official." Mica set her glass down, reached into her pocket, and dropped to one knee. Casey, will you marry me?" She popped open the ring box and held it out to Casey.

"Oh, Mica, it's beautiful. My favorite stone." Casey took the blue star sapphire surrounded by diamonds from the box and handed it to Mica who slipped it on her finger. "Yes, a thousand times, yes."

***

Vacation over, the beaming couple returned home. Casey opened her eyes to find Mica staring at her. She stretched and rolled over to face the woman she couldn't wait to marry. But first, they had to get things settled with their business. "Our big day is here at last for our business. Once this is done, we can turn our attention to our wedding."

The grand opening of the new child care center had finally arrived. They'd hired full-time staff to work with the kids. Some of their older clients had expressed a desire to help with the children, and plans were in the works to integrate them into the program. Grams and Millie were to be on deck to cut the ribbon later that afternoon. One might have thought they'd won the gold medal when Casey and Mica asked them to do the honors.

"As much as I'd like to stay in bed all day, we need to get going." Casey kissed Mica and rolled out of bed. They ran through the shower and got dressed.

Mica was waiting as Casey came downstairs. She gave her a kiss and a small, beautifully wrapped box.

"What's this?"

"A little something to celebrate." Casey peeled back the paper and opened the present to reveal a beautiful, Victorian necklace. The deep-red, heart-shaped ruby was nestled in white gold filigree. "Oh, Mica, it's beautiful. Thank you. Put it on for me?"

Mica hooked the necklace and wrapped Casey in her arms. "I love you."

"I love you, too. I'll save your present for later." Casey wiggled her eyebrows and turned around. "We have to get going. We don't want to be late."

They made the short trip to their physical therapy center, pulled in, and parked. Casey put her hand into Mica's. "I never get tired of looking at it." They had kept the business name, Fit As A Fiddle, although the building bore a larger sign with a new logo.

Together, their attention was drawn to a very pregnant Dr. Eden Brown making her way into the building. Eden had married her boyfriend after she got her degree and was now the managing director of the center.

"Eden's due date is coming up." Casey unlocked her seatbelt. "I pity that poor kid she's having."

"I know. He's going to have all those pseudo grandparents doting on him. Bet his feet won't touch the ground until he's twenty-one."

Casey chuckled. "There is that. Plus, who knew being his godmothers would mean she'd saddle him with our names? Harrison Baxter Brown." She shook her head.

"Like you said, poor kid." They both chuckled.

A small group of senior citizens caught Mica's eye, as they made their way across the road and into the center. "Look. Breakfast time."

They'd started with a small coffee shop in the old building, before they moved. With the senior apartments nearby, the number of clients grew. Lisa worked with them as a consultant, and they'd hired Serena as cook and manager to run the Café. The reputation for good, healthy food began to spread, and people visiting the strip mall would often stop in for breakfast, lunch, or sometimes coffee and a chat.

"We'd better get in there before our nitpicking accountant docks our pay. Trish does like her new power." Mica said, making them both laugh out loud. She glanced at her watch. "In about an hour, I'll go pick up our very own geriatric version of Thelma and Louise for the opening."

They looked at each other with eyes softened by love. "See that empty plot of land over there? Wouldn't it be nice if there could be an assisted living facility?" Casey reached into her pocket and pulled out a twenty-dollar bill. She leaned over and gave Mica a quick kiss. "Maybe when you pick up the deadly duo, you could stop in at the convenience store and buy us a couple of scratch offs."

The End

About AJ Adaire

If you had told me, when I was struggling to write a one page story for my high school writing composition class, that I would one day write seven novels, I would have bet everything that would never happen. No one, especially me, ever considered it a remote possibility. Thirty years later, during a blizzard, having read all the lesbian fiction books I had in the house, I declared to my surprised partner, "I think I could write one of these." So you see, I wrote my first book just to see if I could do it. The completed novel occupied space on my bookshelf, untouched for many years. One day while in a cleaning frenzy, I considered disposing of the neatly stacked and now age-yellowed pages. As I began to read the long forgotten work, I was surprised to discover that the story was enjoyable. Editing and retyping the first book provided a new sense of accomplishment and additional tales followed.

Now retired, I live on the east coast with my partner of twenty-nine years. Because we love a challenge we provide a loving home for two spoiled cats instead of a dog. In addition to writing, any spare time is devoted to editing, reading, mastering new computer programs, and socializing with friends.

Contact Information

If you want to be notified of future releases, please sign up for AJ's newsletter at http://www.ajadaire.com/newsletters/

E-mail: mailto:aj@ajadaire.com
Website: http://www.ajadaire.com
Facebook: http://www.facebook.com/ajadaire
Desert Palm Press: www.desertpalmpress.com

Other books by AJ Adaire

Friend Series

Sunset Island
ISBN: 9781301136629

Ren Madison is certain her life couldn't be more perfect. She owns a private island with an Inn off the coast of Maine. She treasures her loving relationship with her older brother Jack, his wife, Marie, and dotes on her niece Laura. She has a passionate and supportive relationship with her partner, Brooke, and a successful business that doesn't require her undivided attention allowing her ample time to pursue her true passion, painting.
Ren's idyllic world crumbles when Brooke dies. Friends and family worry that Ren may never fully recover from her loss.
Dr. Lindy Caprini, a multi-lingual professor, is looking for an artist to illustrate the book she is writing comparing fairy tales from around the world. To make working together on the book easier, Lindy takes a year sabbatical and leaves friends, home, and boyfriend in Pennsylvania and moves to Ren's island. Ren soon discovers that the beautiful and mischievous Lindy is a talented author and a witty conversationalist. Their collaboration on the book leads to a close, light hearted, and flirtatious friendship. Will their collaboration end there?

The Interim (a novelette)
ISBN: 9781311099051

Devastated that her partner cheated, Melanie flees to a new job in Maine, where she meets Ren Madison. Ren is dealing with issues of her own after losing her partner Brooke in a plane crash
What happens in the interim after one relationship ends and you're really ready to love again? For Ren Madison, Melanie was what happened.
The Interim fills in the details of Ren Madison's life on Sunset Island after Brooke but before Lindy.

Awaiting My Assignment
ISBN: 9781310825248

Bernie was a liar. Amanda learned that much when she caught her lover cheating the first time. Upon discovering a second indiscretion, Amanda vows there will never be another. She leaves the relationship, fleeing to her friend Dana in New York State. While staying at Dana's home, Amanda meets and falls in love with a wonderful woman named Mallory.

Amanda is ready to move on. However, the consistently surprising Bernie isn't finished yet. Amanda learns of Bernie's rudest betrayal yet when she receives a package from her recently deceased ex-lover. A very surprising revelation and one final request are contained therein. The favor comes with a gift that delivers dramatic and life-altering changes, not only to Amanda's life, but to the lives of her closest friends and new partner as well.

Anything Your Heart Desires
ISBN: 978131163912

"Whoa—lesbians!" That was Stacy Alexander's first thought as she observes the group of women in the new shop across the street kiss each other in greeting. Stacy had been staring out her apartment window trying to think of a motive for the death of the character she'd killed off in her mystery novel. Ah ha—extortion! What could be a better reason for the murder of my heroine than being blackmailed because she's a lesbian? Now all I need is a lesbian to teach me about the 'lesbian lifestyle.'

That's where policewoman Jo Martin enters the picture. Jo has two rules by which she religiously lives her life: never get involved with someone already in a relationship and never, ever date a straight woman.

As Jo and Stacy collaborate on the novel, will Stacy want to gain a more intimate knowledge of the topic, and will Jo hold steadfastly to her rules?

Desert Palm Press

The Friends Series Bundle
ISBN: 9781310825780
Sunset Island, The Interim Awaiting My Assignment, and anything Your Heart Desires in an ebook bundle.

Desert Palm Press

One Day Longer Than Forever
ISBN: 9781310847738

Dr. Kate Martin needs a vacation after a failed romance with her business partner nearly ruins her. Lee Foster is recovering from her first lesbian relationship that self-destructed when her partner moved several states away, leaving her behind. Two failed romances, a double booked vacation cabin, and a blizzard—will fate intervene again and turn a passionate affair with a stranger, into something more?

Desert Palm Press

It's Complicated
ISBN: 9781311122964

Victoria Brannigham had a guilty pleasure. Every day she would take a detour, sit on the boardwalk, and wait. She tried not to covet what could never be hers. Beverly McMannis was lonely, until she discovered another lesbian on the island. Bev eagerly embraced the growing friendship with her neighbor. Victoria was honest with Bev right from the start; explaining that she wasn't free to explore their attraction. Bev promised to honor the boundaries. Love isn't always easy, sometimes it's complicated...especially when she doesn't know you're still being faithful.

Desert Palm Press

I Love My Life
ISBN: 9781311310002

Stephanie Kincaid and her friends, Tina and Terry, enjoy sailing Maine's waters. They meet Chris Baxter in a navigation refresher class and quickly become friends. Chris, in need of a place to stay, soon moves in with Stef and friendship gradually grows into romance. Unexpected news about her sister interrupts their sailing vacation along the coast and forces Chris to return and face her past, while Stef remains onboard to help her friends sail back to their home port. What surprises will Chris learn from her ex, her sister, and her family, and how will they change her life?

Journey To You
ISBN: 9781311571854
What do you do if you are one of the few who remain alive after a mysterious, flu-like virus claims most of the global population? This is a question Kim Robins and Peri Henderson have to answer when the world changes and society falls apart. Violent gangs of looters make it unsafe to remain in the city. Hoping to improve their chances for survival, Kim and Peri decide to hike into the remote forest area of Maine. Dangerous circumstances along the trail cause the women to join forces with another hiker and her dog. The longtime friends and their new companions set off on a daunting trek filled with both menacing and kindhearted survivors.
With evidence of the illness everywhere they go, will this journey bring each of the women the happiness and safety she seeks?

Don't Forget
ISBN: 9781311571318
In 1986, Jamie Parker falls in love. What could be bad about that? Nothing except that the object of her affection is Val DiLeona, friend and fellow administrator in the same school district. If Jamie has misinterpreted that Val has similar feelings, confessing her affection could result in the end of their friendship. Then there is the little matter

of the consequences at work. Outing herself as a lesbian could result in her losing her job.

Nearly thirty years later, in 2016, Jamie meets ambulance driver, Kelly, in a hospital waiting room. Upon learning how long Jamie and her partner have been together, Kelly asks Jamie to tell her their story. As Jamie begins, neither woman can imagine the impact their casual conversation will have on their lives, and the lives of those they love.

Note to Readers:

Thank you for reading a book from Desert Palm Press. We have made every effort to edit this book. However, typos do slip in. If you find an error in the text, please email lee@desertpalmpress.com so the issue can be corrected.

We appreciate you as a reader and want to ensure you enjoy the reading process. We would like you to consider posting a review on your preferred media sites such as Amazon, Smashwords, Bella Books, Goodreads, Tumblr, Twitter, Facebook, and/or your blog or website.

For more information on upcoming releases, author interviews, contest, giveaways and more, please sign up for our newsletter and visit us as at Desert Palm Press: www.desertpalmpress.com and "Like" us on Facebook: Desert Palm Press.

Bright Blessings

Made in the USA
Columbia, SC
02 July 2018